In tribute to Edward Said

New war, provok't; our better part remains
To work in close design, by fraud or guile
What force effected not: that he no less
At length from us may find, who overcomes
By force, hath overcome but half his foe.

—John Milton, *Paradise Lost* I, 645–49

Samuel Hazo

The author of books of poetry, fiction, essays, and plays, Samuel Hazo is the founder and director of the International Poetry Forum in Pittsburgh, Pennsylvania. He is also McAnulty Distinguished Professor of English Emeritus at Duquesne University, where he taught for forty-three years. From 1950 until 1957 he served in the United States Marine Corps, completing his tour as a captain. He earned a B.A. magna cum laude from the University of Notre Dame, a M.A. for Duquesne University, and his Ph.D. from the University of Pittsburgh. Some of his previous books are *The Holy Surprise of Right Now* and *As They Sail* (poetry), *Stills* (fiction), *Feather, Mano a Mano,* and *Watching Fire, Watching Rain* (drama), *Spying for God* (essays), and *The Pittsburgh Thats Stays Within You* (memoir). His translations include Denis de Rougemont's *The Growl of Deeper Waters,* Nadia Tueni's *Lebanon: Twenty Poems for One Love,* and Adonis's *The Pages of Day and Night.* His recent book of poems, *Just Once: New and Previous Poems,* received the Maurice English Poetry Award in 2003. A new collection of poems titled *A Flight to Elsewhere* was published in 2005, as was a new prose collection, *The Power of Less: Essays on Poetry and Public Speech.* The University of Notre Dame, from which he received the Griffin Award for Creative Writing in 2005, awarded him his tenth honorary doctorate in 2008. A new book of poems, *The Song of the Horse: Poems 1958–2008* appeared in that same year. A National Book Award finalist, he was chosen the First State Poet of the Commonwealth of Pennsylvania by Governor Robert Casey in 1993, and he served in that capacity until 2003.

THIS PART OF THE WORLD

1

LOW AND SILVER between the dun mountains, the spotter plane hovers in the heat waves like a mirage. Above it the vague clouds slur to the east in whiffs, and the midafternoon sun is already a scrim of gradually purpling horizontals that rise from amber-orange at the horizon to gray-lavender at the zenith. The plane skims less than a hundred feet over the rocky floor of the valley, and the miniature thunder of its motor is all the sound there is. Mile by hovering mile, it keeps coming on like a mountain eagle swooping down from the peaks at dusk on a foray.

This is the third flight in two days for the pilot. Squinting through the last flashes of the sun, he approaches the village at an azimuth different from those of his previous two flights so that the cameraman in the seat behind him can photograph the village and the surrounding area from a new perspective. When he is less than a mile from the village, the pilot suddenly climbs and continues climbing. At the top of his climb, he can survey the entire village from his side window. He nods to his cameraman and then listens to the pleasing and definitive clicks of the shutter as the cameraman works at his command. After the last click, the pilot banks hard right over the center of the village so as to avoid the mountains that contain it as the wings of a stage contain the stage. Looking down at the same overview for the third time in forty-eight hours, he still sees no sign of life, not even a goat or a stray chicken behind the houses. He glimpses what is left of the church, the central square with its water trough, the whitewashed block walls of the houses, many of them roofless, that cover every inch of the plateau. As he circles the two trails that meander from the village down the slope into the valley, the pilot contemplates a final pass, not for more photographs but because he hopes to surprise someone in passage from one house to another. He even hopes that the plane might draw ground fire. He circles. He waits. Nothing. Shrugging, he banks and heads back across the valley. The silver wings of the plane glitter like sheet lightning, and the small noise of the motor ebbs in diminishing echoes into the low silence of the valley and high silence of the mountains.

2

WHEN THE FIRST SOUND of the plane's motor reaches him, the Corsican orders everyone by walkie-talkie to keep from being seen from the air. He then makes a separate call to the guerrillas in the mountains behind and above the village to stay completely out of sight and to refrain from firing at the plane under any circumstances. Then he squats beside his window and peers out over the valley. He glimpses the glinting silver of the plane's wings as it approaches, and he smiles and whispers to himself, "Come closer, keep coming closer, my little sparrow. Take all the pictures you need."

Actually this third reconnaissance in less than two days is disturbing to the Corsican. He tells himself that Caseres is probably taking no chances, that he is preparing as thoroughly as possible, that he wants to be absolutely sure there will not be any surprises. "Very well, Commandante," the Corsican whispers to himself. "Very well, so much the better." This pattern of preparation has been the same in so many past skirmishes that the Corsican knows what to expect even without trying to think about it. The memories of attacks and ambushes in Algeria, Ireland, and the outskirts of Jerusalem think for him. "Yes," he says aloud so that the boy near the door turns as if he is talking to him. "Yes, it will be the same." The Corsican leans back against the wall of the bunker. He folds his arms, which have always seemed too long for his body, and frowns. He has a face that could easily be mistaken for the face of an ascetic—concave cheeks, high and prominent cheek-bones, and aviator's eyes. His lips are but two horizontal lines. He runs his fingers through his thick gray hair and frowns again.

The Corsican looks at the boy, who is returning the look as if he is expecting a command. He notices the harelip that is barely concealed by an adolescent mustache. For some reason he had not detected it when the boy came to him and volunteered to fight in Megiddo. The Corsican had tried to dissuade him, first by laughing at him, then by reasoning, finally by ignoring him. But the boy insisted on staying. He kept saying it was for a personal reason, but he would not tell the Corsican the reason. He added that he would not leave even if he were forced and that a boy of seventeen could pull a trigger as well as anyone else. So the Corsican relented but only on the condition that the boy serve as his messenger and that he remain close to him at all times before, during, and after the battle.

As the plane banks over the village, the Corsican follows its arc and turns again to the boy, who is crouching near the door and spitting at a fixed spot between his boots.

"Do you know what makes spit?" asks the Corsican.

"No."

"Tension," he says and pauses. "Some people who have never known real tension or fear think that tension and fear make your mouth dry. It's just the opposite."

The boy looks at him as if the words have no meaning for him. Then he asks, "When will they come?"

"Tomorrow. Tomorrow at dawn. That's when they always come." The Corsican pauses, then resumes in a lower tone. "Tell me again your name."

"Joseph."

"How many are you in your family?"

"Just my mother and my sister."

"No brothers?"

"Just one sister."

"What is her name?"

"Magdalena."

"Does she know you are here?"

"Tomorrow she will know. I wrote her and told her where I would be. And I told her why."

"Will you tell me why?"

"No."

"Why did you have to write to her?"

"She does not live at home anymore," the boy says and pauses just before he spits again at the spot between his boots. "She lives in the city now. She has her own apartment there."

"What did you say her name is?"

"Magdalena."

3

JOSEPH TRIES TO STOP SPITTING at the now expanding damp
spot between his boots, but the saliva keeps gathering in his
mouth. It was not like that when he visited his sister in the city a
month earlier. His lips then were so dry that they seemed ready
to crack, and he kept swallowing the dry swallow of the sick or
the parched.

There was only one bus a day from his village, and it left at
dawn and stopped at village after village en route to the capital to
pick up other passengers, most of them domestics or street labor-
ers. Everyone aboard the bus was sullen. It seemed to Joseph that
they were like the condemned being trucked to an execution.

He did not come to the capital often. He did not like to leave
his mother alone for that long. Magdalena had tried to persuade
the two of them to leave the village and live in an apartment that
she would find for them in the city, but her mother refused.

"Your father was born and died in this house, Magdalena,"
said her mother as if she were reciting an oath. "You and Joseph
were both born in this house. How can I leave? All of my memories are in this house." She turned to a totally invisible presence in
the room and repeated, "My husband, my daughter, and my son
were born in this house. How can anyone ask me to leave?"

And that ended all thought of moving. Joseph and his mother
would stay in the village, and Magdalena could not change that.
Periodically Joseph would travel to the capital to see his sister or

to bring news from the village or to return with money and dry goods that Magdalena always had waiting for him.

The capital overwhelmed Joseph. At first the traffic frightened him because he was not accustomed to automobiles and trucks. Working with horses in the field or caring for chickens in the village established a completely different rhythm in his life, and the city contradicted that. Having to cope with the rhythm of stopped or moving vehicles was originally beyond him, and it took months for him to learn to cope. He often took detours so that he would not have to cross at intersections. The first time he came to his sister's apartment was an ordeal of confusion, detours and backtracking. But with each succeeding visit he simplified his route until he finally gained the confidence that only knowledge and repetition can create. It was with this same confidence that he found his way to his sister's apartment a month before he joined the Corsican at Megiddo. But that confidence did little to help him face his real reason for coming.

"Joseph," said his sister when she opened her apartment door for him. "I didn't know you were coming. Is something wrong?"

"No," said Joseph. "I just wanted to see you." He paused and then added, "I had to see you, Magdalena."

"What happened to your cheek?"

Joseph covered his cheek with his right hand as he entered the apartment and sat down on the sofa in the living room.

"What happened to your cheek?" she repeated. "Were you kicked by a horse? Did you fall?"

"I was fighting."

"Why? Haven't I always told you not to fight?"

"I had to."

"Who was fighting with you?"

"It was in the village. Some of my friends said things to me. I had to answer them."

"By fighting? Don't you talk to your friends anymore?"

"It was not something I could answer with words, Magdalena."

Magdalena smiled and walked to her brother's side. She put her arm around his shoulder and drew him close to her. Then she leaned down and kissed him on the meandering part in his hair.

"What did they say that was so hard for you to answer except with your fists, Joseph?"

Joseph looked directly at her, and her smile vanished. His bottom lip quivered, and tears began to gloss his eyes. "They said . . . "

"What did they say? What?"

"They said you were the whore of the premier!"

Magdalena withdrew her arm and stepped back as if pushed. Then she took a step forward and slapped Joseph twice on the same cheek—the bruised cheek. Joseph took the blows without flinching. Magdalena's cheeks were crimson.

"Who told you this lie?"

"It doesn't matter."

"Does Mama know about this lie?"

"No. I don't think so. I don't know."

Magdalena began to pace the room like a panther, caged. She snarled one question after another, but none of them was directed at Joseph. "How could anyone say such a thing to my own brother? What kind of devil would do something like that?"

Joseph did not lift his head to watch her. He had the look of a man totally exhausted by some extreme, inescapable labor. Even when she came and stood in front of him, he did not look up at her.

"Joseph," she said. "You don't believe this, do you? Look at me, Joseph. You don't believe them? Tell me you don't believe them."

"I don't want to believe them."

"Joseph, I swear by the Holy Virgin that they are liars. You must believe me. You must not let Mama know about this. It will kill her."

"I know."

"All of my money—all the money I send home to you—comes from my singing. You know that."

"They tell terrible stories about you and the premier, Magdalena."

"Lies! They are liars! They are trying to poison you against me! Can't you see that?"

Joseph began to weep in slow, sickening sobs. Magdalena again put her arms around his shoulders and hugged him until he calmed.

"Have you eaten anything since this morning?" she asked.

After a pause, Joseph shook his head no.

"I'll make something." She released him and started for the kitchen. Before she reached it, she walked into her bedroom and returned with a small, tightly rolled cylinder of money. She forced the money into Joseph's hand. "Take this, Joseph. I know you and Mama need it. Now wait here until I make something for you to eat."

She could not remember how long she was in the kitchen. When she returned to the living room, Joseph was gone. She called his name, then noticed that the apartment door was left open. She looked at the sofa where Joseph had been sitting. The roll of money was on the sofa's arm.

4

MAGDALENA KNOWS THAT THE PREMIER will be late. It is one of his unchangeable habits to keep people waiting for him. What others might regard as tardiness or discourtesy has always been his way of underscoring how important he thinks his presence really is. Magdalena tells herself that she should be used to this by now. She remembers how he once kept a crowd of fifty thousand waiting six hours in the sun for him to speak to them. Many people fainted, but no one left. By the time the premier arrived, everyone in the stadium cheered him as if he were the messiah. She knew that it was this that he wanted his tardiness to achieve, and, of course, it did. He then spoke for more than three hours without ever once glancing at a note. He played the throng like an instrument at the start, and by the time he was an hour into his speech he conducted it like an orchestra, evoking cheers from it at one moment, rage at another, and utter silence at the next. When he finished, he stayed at the podium with his head down as if he wanted the crowd to realize that he had given all of himself to them. He slowly raised his head and listened as fifty thousand voices chanted in volley after volley, "Caseres! Caseres! Caseres! Ca-se-res!"

She looks out of her apartment window at the road he will use. She remembers the last time she saw him two days before. He told her then that the thirtieth anniversary of his premiership would have a special significance. She said she knew there would be a festival at the stadium, but he simply shook his head and smiled as if he knew a secret that no one else knew.

"Magdalena," he said to her, "this will be my monument. It will be a cornerstone for Radames as my successor. The army will be there. The Americans will be there. The field–workers are coming from all over the country to be there. We are providing trucks to make sure they will come. The celebration will be massive. It will be great manifestation." As he spoke, he grew more and more impassioned by what he was describing, and he had to pause. He removed a vial from his shirt pocket. Magdalena knew that he kept his glycerin tablets there. He removed a tablet from the vial and placed it neatly under his tongue. "I think I've turned the tide, Magdalena," he resumed. "The Americans are ready to announce their support on my terms by giving me more planes. Not selling them, mind you, but giving them outright. The only problem that remains is that village on the border, the one that the guerrillas are using as their base. Well, the day before the festival there will be no more village. I've already given orders." He paused. Even though he was breathing heavily, he pulled Magdalena close to him. "On the night before the festival, Magdalena, you and I will have such a night. And I won't need this." He eased the partially dissolved glycerin tablet from under his tongue and spat it across the room.

5

"MAJOR KRONOS?"

Kronos looks up from the map that he has spread like a paper tablecloth on the ground.

"Yes, Lieutenant," he says.

"The men are posted for the night, Major."

"Did you pass my orders that we will attack in the morning at 0500?"

"Yes, Major."

"Good," says Kronos and pats the lieutenant on the shoulder. "Get some sleep then. Carry on."

"Yes, Major."

Kronos watches the lieutenant trudge down the narrow trail to the valley where the entire battalion is bivouacked. He keeps his eyes on him until he reaches his platoon. Then he turns his attention once again to the map on the ground. He has already drawn a circle around the bivouac area and another circle around the village called Megiddo that is the target for tomorrow. He remembers how the premier himself issued the orders in front of the entire battalion two days earlier. He remembers particularly how he and everyone in the battalion waited at attention in the sun until the premier arrived and then waited even longer to allow the premier to inspect each rank of each platoon and then went on waiting while a small riser was brought for the premier so that he could stand on it to address the troops.

Kronos had long been familiar with the premier's preference to let people wait for him. When Kronos had been billeted for a year at the War College in Carlisle, Pennsylvania, he made it a point to note the differences between qualities that Americans responded to in their leaders and those in his own culture. In the United States, a leader was respected primarily on the basis of how much wealth he commanded, both economic and political. That seemed to be primary in that part of the world. Kronos compared that standard to what was respected in this part of the world—his part. A man was perceived as a leader based upon the size of his entourage, his ability as an orator (without notes), and finally by how long people would wait to hear him speak.

Sweating at attention, Kronos watched the premier mount the riser and stand with his hands clasped behind his back. "You have been picked for this mission," said the premier like a man issuing an order, "because you are men who are out of the ordinary. You are professional soldiers in the highest sense. You are dedicated to your country and to its premier. Tomorrow's mission will be of great value to our country, but I must tell you now that it must be a mission of silence. You will do it—and I know you will do it superbly—and then you will forget everything about it. It will not be reported inside the country or outside the country for strategic reasons. But the importance of this battle cannot be stressed sufficiently. Believe and trust your premier when he tells you this, and do your duty like the brave soldiers you are."

When Kronos was assembling the soldiers chosen for the mission, he made sure that he picked the most athletic. In that sense they resembled Kronos himself—men like wrestlers with a low center to their physiques. He needed such men for fighting in the mountains. As he stood behind them and surveyed them in formation, he was satisfied that he had chosen well. The men stood erect and ready to do whatever had to be done.

Kronos remembers how the men saluted Caseres when he left the camp and how the premier, despite the rumors about his heart condition, looked every bit like a field officer in his uniform. In fact, to Kronos he looked fit enough to lead the mission himself.

6

SOLDIERING HAD BEGUN TO LOSE its hold on Kronos. He kept finding too many of his fellow officers who had made an art of "thinking at right angles" or finding ways of impressing those who outranked them. He could name fewer and fewer people with whom he could converse. His wife, the one person in whom he could confide, sensed this and persuaded him to take his annual leave with her out of the country. Since he could find no reason to refuse her, he agreed.

They spent two weeks on the island of Aruba. Each day on the island was almost a repetition of the first day. They swam in the morning, ate a leisurely lunch, eased themselves into the rhythm of the siestas, took long walks on the shore before dinner, read or just talked afterward, and then slept with the windows open and the sound of the sea winds and the Caribbean surf in their ears.

"We're making love the way we did when we were twenty," she said to him one afternoon.

"What do you mean?"

"In the daytime . . . "

He laughed briefly, then stopped and shrugged, realizing that what she had told him was true.

"At home at night," she continued, "we're both so tired at the end of the day that we bring no energy and imagination to one another. That explains a lot, and it took this trip to Aruba to make me realize it. How many arguments have we had late at night?

Too many. And over what? Nothing, really. It's just the tiredness that causes them."

He nodded yes. At a distance like this, the ways they had neglected the important moments in their lives seemed so obvious and correctable that he never wanted the vacation to end.

The day before they were scheduled to return to their country, Kronos and his wife were taking their usual late afternoon walk on the beach when he turned to her and said, "These have been happy days. I didn't think it could turn out like this when we first came here."

"We could have gone anywhere," she answered. "It was just a case of getting away. I could see how tired you were."

"It's not just a question of being tired."

He stopped and looked out to sea. She knew he was assembling his thoughts, and she waited. She prepared herself for . . . she really had no idea what she should prepare herself for, so she just waited, trying all the while to keep her anticipation in check.

"I'm a good soldier, Cristina. I've always been a good soldier. I take pride in that."

"I know that."

"For the past five years I've lost my enthusiasm for the army, for the missions, for the regulations, for everything. The only thing that keeps each day alive for me is working with my men. I know each one of them as if he were my own brother, and they are all the best at what they do. When I'm with them, I forget everything else. They are my reality."

"Doesn't everyone have doubts about life now and then? Why should it be any different for a soldier?" She paused to see if her words were having an effect. "Maybe you'll feel differently when we get back home."

"Did you know that the Chinese poets thought that a soldier was someone to be pitied?"

"No."

"Well, they did. Lately, the more I read and the more I think about what I've read, the more I see that military life is at its core a life of death. A soldier is just an instrument of death."

"But a soldier does what he does for his country. That makes all the difference."

"Death is death," responded Kronos. "I've seen enough of death to know that it's at the bottom of everything. I've never thought about the military this way before. It's made me cautious, not so much for myself as for my men. Losing one of them would be like losing someone of my own blood, like losing a son."

"Do other officers feel this way?

"I don't know one soldier among them, not one real soldier. They're all in training to be politicians. Being in the army is just a preparation for politics for them. They spend half of their time developing a cadre as their future base. They've been trying to get me involved. They say the premier will not live forever. And they have no respect for his son, Radames. They say we should prepare ourselves for the future."

"And how do you answer them?"

"I tell them I'm a soldier. I tell them that a soldier's business is war, not politics, not plotting for this and for that. But even when I listen to my words, I'm not as certain as I used to be about what I am supposed to do, about what I'm doing. I've been reading a lot, thinking a lot." He paused. "I'm thinking of leaving the army, Cristina. Not this year, but soon after that. I think I want to be a teacher. I think I want to teach history."

"You know how history is taught in our country . . . "

"Yes," he answered, shuffling slowly down the beach. "That's the problem."

7

CASERES UNBUTTONS HIS MILITARY TUNIC, removes a glycerin tablet from his shirt pocket and holds it momentarily between his lips like a lifesaver or an aspirin he has not yet decided to taste. Then he works it slowly under his tongue, wincing slightly at the first suck. He does not hear the knock at the door. When the knock is repeated, he re-buttons his tunic.

"Come," he states.

The door is opened, and a younger, shorter, heavier version of Caseres stamps into the office. He is wearing a white sport shirt, riding britches, and gleaming, black boots.

"Where have you been?" asks Caseres.

"Polo."

"What kind of a son are you, Radames? If it's not polo, it's sailing. If it's not sailing, it's racing in that damned Porsche. Is this the way you want to waste your life?"

Despite a certain physical similarity, the differences between Caseres and Radames become more and more obvious as they stand close to one another. Where Caseres is lean, Radames tends toward pudginess. Caseres at six feet three inches is almost half a foot taller than his son. Caseres is clean shaven. Radames has a square patch of mustache trimmed so that the hairs stick straight out like barbs. Caseres walks with an erectness that carries with it a touch of defiance and a sense of command. Radames moves in a kind of lope, his shoulders rolling in time with each step. Caseres' mouth is like a seam or a drawn zipper. Radames has fuller lips, and they are always slightly parted as if to facilitate breathing.

"I'm ready to do whatever you ask me to do," says Radames.

"The first thing I want you to do is to get out of those damn clothes. You look like you're in costume, for God's sake. Where's your uniform?"

"At the villa."

"Get it and meet me in four hours at the stadium. I want to make sure that everything is the way it's supposed to be for Sunday. After that we have a meeting with the Americans. And it's very important. That's why I want you in uniform."

Radames turns to leave. He takes only a few steps toward the door when Caseres calls after him, "When I'm dead, Radames, this country is going to be yours. Remember that."

Radames pauses and then resumes his loping gait to the door.

"Another thing," says Caseres, who waits until Radames is facing him before he adds, spitting out the words, "You're getting too fat."

8

THE CORSICAN WATCHES the dusk engulf the valley like a tidal wave, overwhelming and darkening the peaks, streaming down the slopes, sluicing over the foothills and across the bedrocks and dunes.

"Joseph," calls the Corsican.

The boy turns and looks at the Corsican like a puppy called to attention.

"Make sure the radio's working, Joseph. I want you to call the others and tell them to come here for a meeting in half an hour."

Squinting, the Corsican surveys the entire village and the valley below his parapet. He knows that the American named Hull is at his far right with six men. Flanking him is Sabertes, the priest, with ten men. That leaves him and his twelve men, not counting Joseph, to complete the semicircle.

After the first flight of the spotter plane, the Corsican plotted the firing positions of each of the defenders, concentrating primarily on the fields of fire of the machine gunners (with Hull) and those with automatic weapons and rocket launchers (with Sabertes). After he finished, he was satisfied that there was not an area within the entire village and as far as one hundred yards down the slope to the valley floor that was not covered by crossfire. He had already made sure that the only two entries to the village were placed in enfilade so that any invading soldiers attempting to escape through either entrance could not avoid the bullets or rockets.

As he thinks of the day's work, the Corsican smiles. He remembers how Hull and the others were awed by his knowledge of the terrain as well as of his grasp of the plotted firepower of just thirty-one men.

"Where did you learn about tactics and defense?" Hull asked him when they were alone.

"From the Germans mostly. Their field tactics were always flawless."

"There's more to this than German tactics."

"The rest from Algiers. As for the defensive measures in the village itself—all from Algiers."

"I thought you were going to say Vietnam."

The Corsican knew that Hull was a veteran of Vietnam. "I could never say that. I was never in Vietnam."

"You were lucky."

The Corsican did not know how to deal with Hull. The man seemed to be carrying within him either a private self or an equally private memory, both of which were out of reach of anyone, including himself. The Corsican automatically respected men who kept their own counsel, and his respect for Hull was assured if only for that reason.

"Joseph," the Corsican says to the boy.

Joseph has been checking the terminals of the radio as well as the walkie-talkies. "Everything is working," he says.

"Tell the American and the priest that I want to see them here in thirty minutes."

9

MAGDALENA HEARS THE PREMIER'S MERCEDES, hears it brake to its usual crunching halt on the gravel driveway, hears the car door being opened and closed and then the perfectly spaced boot steps of Caseres on the stairs. She knows the ritual and rhythm by heart. After eight steps, the pause on the balcony landing. After the pause, the sound of the key being inserted in the keyhole. Then the turn of the key, the door being slowly eased open.

When she looks up, she sees Caseres standing in the door-way. He stops there for a moment before he pushes the door shut behind him.

"Magdalena, you look as if you must have been expecting me," Caseres says with a smile. He removes his tunic and flings it loosely over the back of a chair.

"I always expect you."

"I need something cold, something cold but without ice. Ice is bad for me. What do you have?"

"Beer from Mexico."

"Beer is good."

When she returns from the kitchen with a glass of beer, she sees that Caseres is sitting by the window. He is not looking out the window but at her. As she approaches him, he says, "Stop there for a minute—right where you are."

"Why?"

"Because I can see your entire body right through your dressing gown, and I like what I see."

Beer in hand, she waits until he has looked his fill and then brings the beer to him. He takes the beer with his right hand and then coasts his left hand under her gown and up the inner thigh of her right leg just short of the pubis. Magdalena does not move. He keeps his hand there while he drinks his beer, then lets his palm slide slowly down to the back of her knee.

"Radames is a problem to me, Magdalena."

"How?"

"He doesn't understand what is expected of him."

"He's not you. There are not many men like you."

"He must be me. I cannot accept anything less than that." He pauses. "How much longer can I go on? This heart . . . " He taps his chest with his forefinger. "This heart is like a slush pump. I take pills like pistachio nuts. I could go just like that. And when I do, Radames must be ready. Why can't he see that?"

"Maybe you should have sent him to Paris with his mother."

Caseres is silent. For a moment he seems to be elsewhere, and Magdalena watches him in profile and waits. At times like this, she takes an almost erotic pleasure in studying his face. The line from his forehead to the tip of his nose is straight. There is no bridge at all. He reminds her of a Roman emperor profiled on a coin. His thick eyebrows are wild with long, untrimmed white hairs, and the same wild white hairs sprout near the lobes of his ears.

All at once, as if startled, Caseres breaks his concentration. Surprising her in her study of his profile, he asks, "How is your mother?"

"The same."

"And the boy, Joseph?"

"Joseph is a young man trying to be a man in a hurry."

"Does he know about us, about what you mean to me?"

She remembers Joseph's visit, then says, "I can handle Joseph."

Caseres fishes a wad of currency from his shirt pocket and holds it out until Magdalena takes it.

"If that's not enough for this month, then tell me," says Caseres. "There's always more whenever you need it. You know that."

"It's always enough."

Caseres stands and embraces Magdalena. He lets his hand slide down her back to her buttocks, and then he presses her body against his body, and so they remain for a moment, waist to waist. Magdalena waits for the next move, but he releases her and steps back.

"Magdalena, you are as good as bread. I've been too long without you." He turns away from her and retrieves his tunic from the chair where he flung it. Easing his arms into the sleeves, he says, "Tomorrow we will make up for it. Tomorrow night the Americans will be in my pocket. And my headache near the border will be just a bad memory."

"What headache near the border?"

"Megiddo."

"The village? The one that was bombarded? I thought that the entire population left after that."

"I want to make sure it is finished. I don't want the guerrillas to think they can use it as a base. I want it to be nothing but a bare spot on the mountain."

10

HULL ARRANGES HIS WEAPONS—a pistol from Germany, a carbine from the United States, an automatic rifle from Czechoslovakia. He tells himself that it might as well be a morning in Vietnam, and the weapons could easily be a cache that he is helicoptering to an arms depot near the coast. He blinks hard to shatter the memory before it provokes other memories. Then he runs his palm over his utterly hairless scalp from forehead to crown to neck. Another memento from Vietnam. After seven months there on his second tour, every other pilot in his squadron had been shot down. He was assigned to another squadron and continued to fly. The same attrition repeated itself—all pilots lost except him. Then, during a single week, he began to lose his eyebrows, his eyelashes and the hair on his head, his chest, in his armpits and groin. The doctor in Saigon attributed it to nerves and said the hair would grow back. It never did.

The bombardment of Megiddo was unexpected. Remembering it, Hull tries to concentrate on the German pistol as if concentration alone might help him forget what the artillery sounded like and what it did to the village. In reliving a yesterweek that is suddenly as real as the dusk around him, he hears the shells penetrate the walls and roofs of the houses before they detonate. He remembers the screams of those buried in the collapsing houses and then the small cries and whimpers of the children in the village school before the second barrage silences everything. He relives his sprint to the school as the walls collapse again in his memory. He remembers how he dug and rummaged and shifted the blocks of rubble with both hands. Not a child survived. The little girl—Anita—who was his favorite—he sees her again just as he found her—face up, her eyes closed like a child in midnap. Remembering, he lifts her once more, presses her dead cheek against his own and carries her slowly and cautiously to the village plaza that has somehow been spared. One by one be carries all the dead children there. The other villagers help him. Even the guerrillas come down from their caves to help, and all the men together dig a single grave that is the size of the foundation of a small house, and there they lay the children, shoulder to shoulder.

11

AFTER LEAVING HIS FATHER'S OFFICE, Radames stomps to his white Porsche, jerks open the door, slides on to the contoured black leather of the driver's seat and yanks the door shut. He starts the motor and brings it to a maximum roar before he careens down the driveway past the gaping but deferential gate guards to the highway. There he lurches around a truck and veers into the speed lane. He watches the speedometer register ninety kilometers per hour, then ninety-five, then one hundred and five.

A boy in a tattered white sombrero is leading an old man astride a donkey near the berm of a curve less than a hundred yards ahead of Radames' approaching car. A white dog toddles beside the boy. Suddenly the donkey balks, and the boy tugs at the rope that serves as a kind of leash. The white dog begins barking at the donkey. The dog keeps barking as it backs on to the highway. The boy notices the oncoming Porsche and shouts at the dog, but the dog is too busy barking to heed. Seconds later the Porsche's left bumper and tire strike the dog broadside. The dog is sucked under the car at the same instant that it sideswipes the boy, spinning him into a dip in the berm. The boy instinctively tries to stand. He is still holding the donkey's leash. He actually stands fully upright for a moment before his left leg buckles under him, and he falls disjointedly to the ground.

Radames has not stopped because of the accident. Instead he accelerates, and in seconds he is out of sight. The old man on the donkey watches the white Porsche disappear down the highway. Then he dismounts and runs to the boy while the donkey sidles to the grass fringe of the berm and begins to nibble the grass. The old man turns away from the boy, starts toward the donkey, stops, returns to the boy, then heads again for the donkey before he drops to his knees and presses both hands to his temples. He begins to sway and whimper softly. The donkey pays no attention to him. Even after a crowd begins to gather at the scene, the donkey goes on tugging at the grass and chewing.

12

SABERTES KEEPS REMINDING HIMSELF not to play the priest in front of his men. When he decided to come to Megiddo, he burned his collars, his breviaries, his scapulars, and finally his two cassocks. Still his reputation preceded him, and many of the men assigned to his command addressed him as "Father" until he made it clear that he wanted them to call him by his family name, Sabertes. Now as he watches these same men at the sites where the Corsican posted them earlier, he wonders what he will do when the attack comes—issue commands and fight the attackers or else attend to the wounded and the dying like a chaplain? It strikes him as ironic that his command post is located in the ruins of Megiddo's only church. It had not been intentional on his or the Corsican's part, but the coincidence still makes him smile. He, Hull, and the Corsican had drawn lots to determine who would defend certain areas of the village, and he just happened to draw the defense of the center. When he and the Corsican positioned the men, he felt as if they were handing out civic assignments—"You, beside the fountain"—"You, near the far wall of what's left of the school"—"You, opposite the butcher shop."

Megiddo reminded Sabertes of his own village. He knew it well as a boy, and as a priest he came to know and understand it more. After he finished his seminary studies and was ordained, his bishop assigned him to his home parish because he alone of all the newly ordained priests could understand the dialect. He accepted the assignment as providential and ministered to the parishioners there for more than five years. It was after the fifth year that the resistance to Caseres began. Anti-government posters and graffiti appeared on the walls of houses and other buildings during the night. Telephone lines between army installations were mysteriously cut. Later, suspects from the village were taken into custody. For the most part, the suspects were young men. They would be returned weeks or months later, telling of tortures that Sabertes initially believed were exaggerations.

One night he was asked by soldiers from the neighboring army outpost to accompany them in order to anoint a dying prisoner. By the time he was taken to the prison hospital, the man was dead, but Sabertes anointed him provisionally. When he touched the man's eyes with holy oil, he noticed the bluish-black marks on his cheeks, the swollen ears, the lips blue and bitten by teeth that were no longer there.

After he finished the ritual with the corpse, Sabertes was led by the soldiers to the prison where several men from the village had been taken. The soldiers said they were examples of how the government treated men who opposed Caseres. Sabertes saw a farmer he knew. The farmer shouted to him as he passed that his eyelids were stitched open so that he could neither blink nor sleep. He lay naked and supine, and Sabertes saw that his scrotum was as large and red as a pomegranate. Sabertes turned to the soldiers and demanded to be taken to the administrator of the prison. The soldiers simply smiled and led him to the gate. When Sabertes paused there and refused to leave until he saw the person in charge, the soldiers pushed him through and out.

"But I must protest this treatment," shouted Sabertes.

"Go back to your church, you," said one of the soldiers, pushing him so that his glasses fell to the floor. "You've done what you were asked to do."

"That man was dead before you sent for me. Why did you want me to come here?" asked Sabertes, retrieving his glasses and putting them on again. He was almost a foot shorter than the soldier, who regarded him with a mixture of scorn and pity.

"Go back and tell the others what is waiting for them when we catch them. Tell them how we deal with traitors. When we tell them, they think we are lying. When you tell them, they will believe you. Now get out."

For nights after that, Sabertes could not sleep. After a week he made a special trip to the capital to see his bishop, but he returned to his village unsatisfied.

"Your duty, my son," the bishop had told him, "is to meet the spiritual needs of those in your parish. Your duty as a priest is to souls, not causes. We cannot be distracted by the merely temporal. This new theology of liberation is a way of distracting us from our mission as priests. We cannot become political. We cannot take sides. We must look always at the eternal."

Sabertes' real conversion began on his return from the capital. He felt himself becoming two persons—one whose feelings and conscience could never again be what they once were, and the other who tried to subordinate these to his ministry. For months he tried to reconcile the two. But each time a prisoner would be returned to the village from the prison with new tales of torture and brutality, Sabertes found the reconciliation more and more difficult. He prayed daily before the altar for an answer. He even fasted and otherwise deprived himself of comforts, hoping that in denial he would be given guidance. One morning, without informing his bishop, his family, or his housekeeper, he left his parish.

13

THE LONGER THAT MAJOR KRONOS studies the map he has grounded in front of him, the more uneasy he becomes about the plan of attack. True, the first two reconnaissance flights had shown that there were no signs of life in Megiddo. But Kronos knows from his own experience in such matters that a camera does not and often cannot capture everything. What if the camera simply could not photograph soldiers who were well hidden in the village? What if the soldiers in hiding were there to repulse any new attack and knew exactly what was required to do so in military terms?

If his assumptions are without basis, Kronos knows that the plan of attack marked out on the map is precisely the one to be followed. Two salients will enter the village simultaneously from two different points. One company will remain in reserve in case of any miscalculation or counterattack. But if his assumptions about the possibility of soldiers in concealment are true, Kronos fears that Megiddo might not be the easy victory that Caseres said it would be when he spoke to the attack force the day before in the staging area.

Peering at the map, Kronos sees it now not as paper and configurations but as actual terrain. The approach to Megiddo from his present position is the flat floor of a valley. For a distance of almost two miles, the soldiers will proceed through the valley bed and mount the gradual slopes to the plateau of Megiddo. On the slopes, they will be completely exposed to enfilade fire from higher ground. Kronos realizes that that will be the most precarious moment. Once the troops gain the plateau, they will invade the village through its only two points of entry, and each of the entry points is no wider than a cart so that the men will have to come through at no more than two at a time.

Kronos folds the map carefully, then swears and slams it to the ground. Staring across the darkened valley at the Megiddo plateau in the distance, he can barely discern the dull white of the few squat houses left standing. Behind and above the village loom the mountains, so for a moment Megiddo strikes Kronos as a carefully chosen nest protected by the double shields of the wings of a giant eagle. He understands completely why this mission has been made the responsibility of ground troops. The artillery had done the preliminary work only days before, but no amount of shelling could ever be as thorough as infantry assaults. That was one of the first things Kronos learned as a field officer.

What was true for artillery was also true of air strikes. They would be helpful but not decisive. Moreover, pilots would find it extremely hazardous to make bombing or strafing runs. Coming in across the valley, they would have to hit their targets and then pull up immediately to avoid colliding with the enclosing mountains. The pilot of the reconnaissance plane had confirmed that, stating that he could have the village photographed only during a quick overflight before he had to veer away from the lower ridges and the slopes.

"Thermopylae," Kronos mutters to himself. "Thermopylae all over again. Thermopylae with no air cover. What if they're waiting for us? What if they planned it this way?"

Kronos remembers the details of the orders that came directly from the premier. There would be no air cover unless it became absolutely necessary, and the premier thought that this would be unlikely. Should there be a defense of the village by any insurgents, the insurgents would be "removed." No prisoners were to be taken. Finally, every structure in Megiddo would be reduced to rubble.

14

FOR HULL, Vietnam and Megiddo blur into one another, not so much as places as states of mind. In Vietnam he had come to live each day as if it could turn out to be his last. Each mission that he survived became nothing but a reprieve for him. Unlike other pilots, he never counted his missions. It always came as a total surprise to him when he was told that he had completed the required number and was entitled to be rotated. For him the war was simply a place where he had to do the job he was trained to do. He did not think too deeply about it because that would have affected his ability to do his job. The politics involved became more and more of an enigma to him.

Now as he thinks about the battle for Megiddo that will happen at dawn, he tastes the venom of Vietnam all over again. The only difference now is that he hates the warrior he feels himself becoming almost against his will. For months after he left Vietnam and was released from active duty, he tried to bury the man in him who had flown missions over the delta, who had strafed the slopes and jungles for soldiers he was told were there, who had smeared the villages and valleys with napalm and Agent Orange. On each of the dawns of those days of his life as a pilot, he would wake and try like Pilate to wash the war off his hands. It was not that he had any scruples about the war—not then, at any rate. It was the daily diet of destruction and the deaths that destruction surely caused that wearied him. Even though he never saw an enemy at close quarters, he knew the capabilities of the ordnance he carried on each mission and the effect this would have on forces on the ground. But month after month it wearied him to think of it. He felt himself growing cold and numb at his core, less able to feel, to respond, to smile.

It was the rescue that changed him completely and irrevocably. After ground fire had struck his plane, he was forced to jettison. Luckily he parachuted near the sea where he was picked up by a helicopter stationed off the coast for just that purpose. The helicopter was also ferrying a South Vietnamese lieutenant and two prisoners back to Da Nang. The prisoners were squatting side by side in the rear of the helicopter, their hands tied with wire behind their backs. One of the prisoners was blindfolded. The lieutenant began questioning the prisoners as the helicopter skimmed southward along the coast. Occasionally the lieutenant would kick one or the other of the prisoners in the ribs or above the ear with a unique, oriental viciousness to show he meant business. Neither of the prisoners said a word or uttered a sound of any kind after being kicked. Hull could see that the lieutenant was not only frustrated but embarrassed in the presence of an American pilot. Suddenly he dragged the blindfolded prisoner toward the open hatch of the helicopter. Holding the man by the hair, he turned to the other prisoner and repeated the same question he had been asking him, but this time he added a sentence or two. The expression of the prisoner who was not blindfolded changed from grim to grimmer, but he still said nothing. The lieutenant's response was to push the blindfolded prisoner out of the helicopter.

For Hull, the prisoner was there, and suddenly he was gone. It happened so quickly that for a moment he did not believe it. When the lieutenant looked at Hull and smiled and shrugged, Hull cursed him in English and then in French. The lieutenant continued to smile and shrug, then turned his back on Hull.

Later, after the helicopter landed, Hull reported the incident to his commanding officer, who shrugged just as the South Vietnamese lieutenant had shrugged. Then he said, "In the language of your run-of-the-mill grunt, what the fuck's the difference? You kill them on the ground with bullets or bombs or napalm. So what if this gook pushes one out of a helicopter from 500 feet? The mission is to knock off as many as possible. Either way you do it, it's one less."

That meeting revealed the war to Hull as he had never permitted himself to think of it. Prior to that, he had looked on his missions simply as assignments. All at once he saw himself as nothing but an instrument in a strategy that had no more exalted purpose than the arithmetic of accumulated murders committed by any means.

15

THE CORSICAN KNOWS that he should sleep if only for the thirty or so minutes that he has before his meeting with Hull and the priest. But the will to sleep is missing. He feels a familiar, deep exhilaration that he always feels before a battle.

Having sent Joseph to inform the guerrillas in the mountains above Megiddo that he has covered every point of entry and exit to the village as well as every open space in the village with intersecting fields of fire, he told the boy to caution them to save their mortar barrages for the enemy's inevitable retreat down the slope and through the valley. There the shells would catch the soldiers in the open.

The Corsican removes a cigarette from his tunic and holds it limply between his dry lips. He leaves it there, unlighted. It is Rafferty's rule—when you have to wait, suck on a pebble or keep a cigarette between your lips. The Corsican imagines that he is with Rafferty again. It is back in a dark alley in Armagh, and he is asking Rafferty why he doesn't concentrate on the British soldiers and leave the civilians alone. And Rafferty's answer is "Because nobody gives a damn when a soldier is killed. It's expected that soldiers will die. There's no revulsion, no surprise. But nobody thinks it's right that civilians should die. According to the rules, they're not supposed to die. And that's why we put our bombs where we put them. In cars. In pubs. In markets. That's what puts our whole cause in the headlines of all the newspapers in the world. It gets us notice." The Corsican remembers with a wry smile that Rafferty was finally killed in an ambush near Armagh by the very soldiers he bypassed to get to the "enemy that's not in uniform."

The Corsican flips the cigarette into the darkness and remembers how he left the IRA and joined the Maquis in occupied France in the last years of the war where he learned how to dynamite bridges and railroad crossings, to ambush, to fight and then fade into the countryside. By the time the Americans finally invaded France and began driving the Nazis back into Germany, the Corsican had killed seventy-six Germans by his own personal count, including one general. Because they admired both his prowess and his ruthlessness, the leaders of the Maquis made him a group commander. He and his men continued to harass the retreating Germans in advance of the regular armies. This was the kind of war that the Corsican preferred, professional versus professional. It was waged without quarter but always by men on both sides who knew exactly what they were doing and why. That seemed honorable to the Corsican because what bothered him wherever he fought was the way military operations almost inevitably had civilian casualties. When he later joined the resistance in Algeria, the same consequences occurred. It was Rafferty's kind of war all over again but with renewed ferocity. In France, if a German patrol were ambushed, the German authorities on the following day would take hostages from the town or village nearest to the ambush on the theory that adjacency was synonymous with complicity. In Algeria even that kind of logic was absent.

His experiences in Algeria showed him how far barbarism could go. The legionnaires, predominantly Germans who had enlisted in the French Foreign Legion after the war because soldiering was literally all they knew and since many had no families to return to in Germany, did not even need the pretext of complicity to execute Algerians. As the situation grew more and more desperate and more embarrassing for them in the country, they would pick any passing civilian as a target of opportunity. This was why the Corsican took a particular pleasure in capturing legionnaires and an even greater pleasure in interrogating them. In captivity, the legionnaires were not the same men. It was one thing for these legionnaires in platoons to regard their Algerian enemies as mere animals marked for extermination. It was something else when, captured and at the mercy of these same "animals," they had to face the men they had been accustomed to regard as subhuman. The Corsican secretly enjoyed seeing how the scorn of the legionnaires began to change, sometimes slowly, at other times quickly, but in most cases—except for one or two stubborn exceptions—inevitably as the interrogation proceeded. For the stubborn exceptions the Corsican reserved a particular hatred since they personified for him the kind of overlord that he saw himself commissioned to defeat and even eliminate from the very earth. From Ireland to France to Algeria and later to Palestine, it was for him the same war. The locales and the languages changed, but the enemy was always the same.

The Corsican had long since stopped asking himself why he continued to do what he did or why he felt a visceral and at times uncontrollable hatred for the men he opposed. He knew he would never change, so he stopped thinking about it and went on.

16

IT IS ALMOST DUSK when Radames reaches his villa. He steers
his Porsche through the electronically controlled main gate and
parks deliberately askew beside the swimming pool. In the late
sun, the pool is as clear and still as muscatel in a glass. Radames
vaults out of the car, looks briefly at the slightly dented fender
where a smear of blood is drying maroon, and strides to the end
of the pool where the water is deepest. Without taking his eyes
off the surface of the pool, he shucks off his boots and socks, then
his trousers and undershorts, and finally his shirt. For a moment
he waits, studying the foreshortened image of his nakedness in
the water. Then he dives in noisily. The entire pool erupts around
his plunge, and the surface wrinkles with ripple after expanding
ripple. Radames breaststrokes to the opposite side of the pool and
climbs out. He strides to the porch of the beach cabana behind
the pool, locates a towel on the back of one of the chairs, and proceeds to dry himself in sure, slow strokes. Just as he finishes, he
hears someone shuffling silverware and dishes inside the cabana.

"Porfirio?"

A moment later a tall, oriental-looking black in a white tunic
and white trousers appears at the door.

"Yes, sir," says Porfirio, completely ignoring the fact that
Radames is naked.

"I left my clothes at the far end of the pool. Take them with
you when you go to the villa and then lay out my uniform."

40

"Yes, sir, I will do it now."

Radames kilts himself with the towel and knots the loose ends at his navel. "Isn't it late for you to be cleaning up, Porfirio?"

"Yes, sir, but I had to wait for everyone to leave first."

"How long ago was that?"

"Late this afternoon, sir, just before you left for your polo match." Porfirio pauses and then says, "One of the women is still here. She is sleeping here in the cabana."

"Sleeping?"

"Yes, sir."

"Very well," says Radames, "I'll deal with her myself. Leave everything here as it is for now and make sure my uniform is ready. I need it for this evening."

"Yes, sir," answers Porfirio and walks at attention to the end of the pool where he picks up Radames' boots and clothing in a clump and carries them to the villa. Radames watches him. Then he shifts his gaze to the mesmerizing surface of the pool, which has leveled now into its former stillness, and walks slowly to the cabana and enters. Momentarily he sees nothing. He is about to turn on the lights when he hears a woman's voice.

"I've been waiting for you, Radames."

"Lily?"

"Yes."

"What are you still doing here?" he asks as he turns on the lights. "I thought you'd be gone hours ago."

"I just told you. I've been waiting for you. Now turn off those lights."

He does as she asks. As his eyes become more and more accustomed to the darkness, he begins to see her in focus. She is seated with her legs tucked under her on the daybed opposite him. He notices that she is wearing only a pair of blue shorts. She slides off the daybed and dances to a rhythm of her own humming as she approaches him. He turns away from her, but she follows him, still dancing and humming and finally grazing his back with her breasts. He stops, and she embraces him from behind so that her hands meet just above the towel ends that he has knotted loosely at his waist.

"Which way shall my hands go, Radames? North? Or south? I know a lot of tricks in the south."

Radames pull her hands apart and faces her.

"Get out of here, Lily. I have to go back into the city. I have no time."

Lily smiles for a moment before she realizes that he is serious. "Are you telling me to leave, to get out?"

"Out. Now."

"What happened to you since this afternoon? You're not talking to one of your whores, Radames. I'm not used to this kind of talk from you or anyone else."

"Get out, Lily. Porfirio will drive you back."

17

PORFIRIO OPENS THE BACK DOOR of Radames' Bentley for Lily as she approaches the car. She flings in her overnight bag.

"Believe me, Porfirio," she mutters, "if I had my own car, I wouldn't bother you to drive me home. I want nothing to do with him anymore." She turns toward the villa and screams, "Do you hear me, Radames? I want nothing to do with you! Nothing! Ever! I spit on you and everything you stand for! I spit on your mother! I spit on your father!"

She waits for some response. Porfirio is standing at attention beside the open door. He acts as if he has heard nothing.

Lily reaches down, comes up with a handful of gravel, and flings it all at the villa. Then she hurls herself into the back seat of the Bentley as Porfirio closes the door behind her.

Before they reach the sea road that leads to the capital, Lily is rapping with the heel of her shoe on the glass partition that separates her from Porfirio. Porfirio reaches across with his right hand and slides open a small window in the partition.

"Porfirio, turn on the air conditioning. I can't breathe back here."

"It will become cooler soon, Madam. The temperature control will . . . "

"I want it cooler now. I'm suffocating in this damn car, his car! Why do you do what *he* tells you to do right away, and you don't do what I tell you to do right away?"

"Madam . . . "

"Don't 'Madam' me, you snake. You're just like him. You enjoy seeing him treat me like this. I know you do. I can read it in your face. You're no better than he is. You're both sons of bitches, sons of whores! You should be more of a man! But all you ever do is what he tells you to do!" She is screaming as she finishes. She sits back in the seat, remembering what happened the night before. Radames had asked her to stay at the villa for the weekend. She had agreed and come with a friend named Rita. Radames told them that he was hosting a few special guests and that two of the Danish dancers from the casino were going to appear around midnight and give them a fashion show.

"A fashion show?" asked Lily.

"You'll see," said Radames.

"Are they blondes?" asked Rita with a grin.

"You are correct as always, Señorita Rita," said Radames. He enjoyed the roll of the rhymes when he pronounced her name like that. He smiled at her. Rita smirked slightly, implying that she no longer found the rhymes amusing. "I have been told that the dancers are both blondes."

"That explains it," said Rita. She turned to Lily and added, "They see so much dark skin and dark hair around here that they are hungry for blondes and light skin. Or should I say light meat? Blondes drive them crazy."

Rita had a reputation for candor, both in public and privately. And her tone of voice was the same in both circumstances. She rarely said anything privately that she would not eventually say out loud, regardless. She was one of those women who could not whisper.

Radames' special guests turned out to be two marine sergeants from the security detachment at the American Embassy. They were escorted by an officer whom Lily immediately recognized as Radames' closest friend and, in fact, his bodyguard. He was taller than Radames by half a foot, had a completely shaven pate and gave the constant impression that he was smiling even when a smile was not expected.

"Thank you, Ramón, for bringing our two American friends. We are always happy to host the United States Marines. Welcome, my friends, to the Villa Alta," said Radames with something of a bow.

The marines looked vaguely uncomfortable, but they responded to Radames' handshakes and soon afterward accepted the piña coladas that Porfirio brought for them.

"We expect to have a very enjoyable evening, gentlemen. I've invited two of the artistes from the casino to give us a private fashion show later. A real fashion show," said Radames, smacking his palms together as if he were sealing a deal. "Nothing is too good for the marines."

Ramón had disappeared into the dressing room in the cabana. He emerged in white bathing trunks, dove unhesitatingly into the pool, and stroked several complete lengths before he paused at the deep end and treaded water calmly.

"If you would like to join me, gentlemen," Ramón said to the marines, "there are bathing suits put aside for you inside the cabana. Feel free. The water is delicious."

"Yes, feel free," repeated Radames.

The sergeants looked furtively at one another. The invitation was obviously a complete surprise to them.

"What do you say, George?" said one to the other. "Are you ripe for a dip?"

"Why not?" George answered, and the two marines headed for the cabana.

Lily and Rita and Radames eased themselves into beach chairs beside the pool and watched Ramón resume his swimmer's laps.

"What do you have up your sleeve, Radames?" asked Rita.

"Insurance. Just insurance, Rita," said Radames with a smile.

"What kind of insurance?

"When you deal with the Americans as we do, it's good to have friends in the right places. In the embassy, for example."

"Why did you invite Rita and me? What are we doing here?" asked Lily.

"You're here as observers. Or shall I say witnesses?"

"Is that all?"

"That depends on you, Señorita Rita . . . "

"I don't like the sound of that any more, Radames. Just call me Rita. That's my name."

"I like the sound of Señorita Rita," said Radames with his usual smile as he stood. "But now I think I'm going to enjoy the refreshing coolness of my swimming pool." He strode to the dressing room just as the two marines were emerging. They were wearing white bathing trunks.

Within fifteen minutes, Ramón, the two marines, and Radames were cavorting in the water like collegians on a vacation.

"Look at them, Lily," said Rita. "They're like boys." She paused. "Sometimes that's all I think that men are . . . grown-up boys. Most of the time they're not even grown up. And we're just their toys. Toys for boys. Isn't that something to think about?"

"I thought you didn't like rhymes."

"In this case the rhymes work."

"Well, I'm not a toy, so speak for yourself, Rita."

"You really are, but you won't admit it."

"Sometimes I think you talk too much."

"Maybe I do, but at least I'm honest when I talk. Look at this whole country. It's run by men for men. All the rules are rules made by men for men. All the businesses are run by men. The government is a private men's club. The army is no different. Why don't you admit it?" She paused to give Lily a chance to respond, but Lily remained silent. "And we just go along with it. We make it possible. We women. We feed them. We give them a home. We give them children. We let them treat us like carpets. They need us for their egos, their stomachs, and that thing they have just below their stomachs. All I have to do to make a man pay attention to me is reach him in one of those three ways—usually the last one."

"You're too bitter, Rita. You're bitter about everything. And you always want to change things because you don't like things as they are."

"The way things are makes me bitter." She watched the men in the pool as if they were targets on a range. "Radames has everything planned for tonight. He's going to get those marines so relaxed that they'll forget they're marines. Then he's going to feed them to these so-called artistes. And after that he'll have them where he wants them."

"You give Radames too much credit for intelligence, Rita."

"He's not intelligent. He's just clever. And for him that's more valuable. When you were ten years old, Lily, you were more intelligent than he is now, more intelligent than he'll ever be. But what good is your intelligence here if you're a woman? What can you do with your intelligence? Even my mother knew that this was a man's country and that intelligence in a woman didn't matter. She was hoping I'd be a boy because she knew what kind of a life was waiting for a woman in this country. She wore black for weeks after I was born."

Rita fished a cigarette and a pad of matches from her purse. After propping the cigarette between her lips, she lit it and smoked in quick, abrupt puffs for a moment. "Last week I tried to name one woman in this whole damn country who was really a woman, and I could name only one, just one."

"Who was that?"

"Magdalena. That singer, Magdalena. She is treated with real respect, especially by men but also by women. And the rest of us? Slaves. Just slaves, when you think about it. We fit into the pattern that these damn men create for us. We're never consulted. We just fit in." She paused and smoked. "And from what I've heard lately, even Magdalena has joined us. The premier from all reports just wants her for himself. So there you are. She's no different from all the rest of us. We matter for nothing. We influence nothing. We make nothing happen except in bed."

While Rita was speaking, the two dancers from the casino were being ushered by Porfirio toward the table where Rita and Lily were seated. Seeing them, Radames hauled himself out of the pool and, smiling broadly, greeted them and steered them toward two beach chairs near the table. Both women were wearing knee-length capes, one black and the other the color of blood. Each wore a small turban that matched the color of the cape.

"Lily. Rita," said Radames. "I'd like you both to meet Astrid and Ingrid."

The two dancers smiled as they seated themselves. When Rita heard Radames pronounce their names, she laughed a single, staccato laugh.

"Astrid and Ingrid are from Denmark," Radames was saying. "They speak only Danish."

"So we can say whatever we want, and they won't understand a word we're saying," said Rita, snuffing out her cigarette. She smiled at both dancers and, still smiling, said, "I can smell you from here, dear Scandinavians. You smell like merchandise."

The dancers simply smiled in return. Radames was not pleased, and Lily looked warningly at Rita, who was not looking at her at all. Lily then concentrated on the dancers. They were still wearing their stage makeup. The lines of their eyebrows were arched and exaggerated, and their lipstick made their lips almost twice as large and wide as they were. Some kind of powder on their upper eyelids made them sparkle.

During this time Ramón and the two marines emerged from the pool and came to the table. After introductions, they took

their seats on the remaining three beach chairs. The dancers nodded and smiled at the men, and Radames waited until Porfirio
brought piña coladas for everybody.

"Now," he said, speaking like an impresario, "I've told our
lovely friends from Denmark that I have special guests from
the great United States Marine Corps tonight. And they asked
if they could present in honor of our guests the same fashion
show that they present each night at the casino." He turned
and began speaking to the dancers in what sounded like bad
French to Rita.

"I thought they spoke only Danish, Radames," said Rita
sarcastically.

"That's right," said Radames, "but they know some French.
And some Turkish."

Rita leaned toward Lily and said, "The Turks like white
meat also."

Lily watched as the two dancers stood and walked side by
side to the far end of the pool. They conversed briefly there in
whispers, then separated and began a slow, dancer's walk back
to the table, one on one side of the pool, and the other on
the opposite side. They walked now almost like models, their
faces expressionless but slightly sullen, their focus on a horizon
only they could see, their steps elongated so that they seemed to
glide. As they neared the table, they swirled out of their capes
simultaneously. Each was wearing a body suit. The one with
the black cape wore a red suit, and the one with the red cape
wore a black one. Each suit fit as snugly as skin. As they glided
closer, Lily noticed that the suits covered every part of each
woman's body except those parts that were normally concealed.
The breasts protruded peepingly through two circular openings, and a larger circle revealed the women's navels and pubises
and, when they turned around, their naked buttocks up to the
small of the back.

The marines looked at one another and smiled. Radames noticed their looks and nodded toward Ramón. The dancers paced back and forth for several moments longer, then broke their poses and returned to the table.

"They're not blonde all the way down, Radames," said Rita, grinning.

The marines were now totally under the spell of the dancers, who had not bothered to reclaim their capes. The dancers sipped daintily what was left of their drinks through straws and knowingly let the marines consume them with their eyes. Rita could see that the "insurance plan" was working as Radames intended. It would only be a matter of time before Radames would ask to be excused so that he could show the dancers the villa. Then Ramon would find some reason to take the marines inside. Then Radames would return alone to Rita and Lily.

After the script evolved as Rita imagined it would, she said to Radames, "I presume that Porfirio has his camera loaded and ready to take some revealing photographs for use later, Radames."

"Señorita Rita, I could not have said it better myself."

"You act and even look like a pimp, Radames," said Rita.

"And if I am, what does that make you?"

"Accomplices, I suspect."

"If our families were not related, Rita," said Radames, "I would not tolerate your insults for a second." With that he turned his back and headed for the pool.

Lily and Rita watched him after he dove into the pool and began swimming, noting that he swam as he lived, cumbersomely but always slowly moving ahead.

"Why do you always go out of your way to insult him and make him angry?" asked Lily. "We didn't come here to fight."

"I can't help myself. Sometimes I feel if I don't say something, I'll choke."

From the interior of the villa came the sound of soprano laughter. Then there was a slow sentence in French spoken with a Danish accent. This was followed by the voice of one of the marines—"If that's the way you want it, sister, you won't get a fight from this Kentucky boy."

"Well," said Rita, "everything seems to be going according to plan."

"Don't you think you should apologize?"

"For what? For telling the truth?"

"I think you should, regardless. Radames can be nice when he wants to, Rita. And he has influence. You never know when you might need him."

"You're sounding as clever as he is, Lily. You're thinking just the way he thinks." Rita stood. Her expression showed that she had come to a decision. "All right, you want me to apologize? I'll apologize. I'll apologize my way. Watch me. I want to prove something to you. Just don't interfere. It's not what is said that makes a difference. It's what is done. So watch."

Radames was watching as well. He stood in waist-high water and watched as Rita removed her dress and her underthings, walked with a will to the diving board, and posed there for a moment. Her entire body glistened in the pool-reflected light of the mosquito bulbs. The sound of the mosquitoes hitting the bulbs and sizzling when they hit had been in the background during the entire evening.

"Do you like my personal fashion show, Radames?" Rita called out over the water.

Radames smiled and waved to her.

"This is the way we do a fashion show in this country, not in Denmark. We get right to the point," said Rita, still posing.

Radames did not take his eyes away from her as she dove cleanly into the pool and swam like a shadow underwater until she burst the surface just in front of him. Radames reached for her and started to pull her toward him.

"Why are you in such a hurry, Radames? We have all night."

Lily remained in her chair while Radames and Rita wrestled in a mock struggle in the shallow water. Periodically Rita would look in Lily's direction and smile. At one point Rita went to the side of the pool and attempted to pull herself up, but Radames caught her and splashed her back into the pool. Lily had the feeling that Rita wanted to be caught, that this was part of whatever strategy she had in mind, that whatever frictions existed between Radames and Rita were being neutralized in the game that Rita was playing with him in the water. And that, Lily suddenly realized, was precisely the point that Rita wanted Lily to see, and that the only way she could make her see it was to become in total nakedness the woman that Radames wanted her to be to suit his purposes.

Finally, Rita did free herself long enough to sit on the lip of the pool, her toes making small circles on the surface, her thighs parted just enough to let Radames see between. When Radames half-waded and half-swam toward her and held her right foot in in his hand, Rita said, "Give me one minute to go to the bathroom, Radames. I can't help it. I have to. Let me go. I'll be right back."

"Don't be long," said Radames.

Rita stood and walked toward Lily. Radames was swimming away from the edge of the pool where she left him. When he turned on his back, Lily could see that his eyes were closed, and his hair was parted in the middle by the water.

Rita gathered her dress and underwear in one armful.

"I'm leaving, Lily," she said. "I'm taking the car. You can come if you want to. If not, you'll have to get back on your own. I can't stay here a minute longer."

"You mean you're leaving now?"

"Right now."

"What was that all about in the pool?"

"A biology lesson. No, it was a political lesson. You can have him if you want him. He doesn't want me. All he wants is a woman. He's big as a bull in there now. I could feel him against me." Rita could see that Lily was not going to leave. "I'm going. I'll talk to you tomorrow. I'll dress in the car."

The laughter from the villa was growing louder. Lily listened to it as she watched Rita exit through the shrubbery to the spot where she parked her car. Radames, his eyes still closed, was backstroking in wider and wider circles in the water.

18

HULL CAN STILL SEE THE MOUNDS where he and the others had buried the children after the barrage. All the children of Megiddo—gone. During his entire life Hull had been able to come to terms with anyone's death, but he could never resign himself to the death of children. Not being a believer, he could not find providential meanings in their passing. His only defense was to work with the children who were left alive. While he was in college, he had worked with children as a camp counselor during the summers. Then Vietnam had happened, and he promised himself that he would return to this same work after his discharge.

In order to keep himself from losing his mind in Vietnam, Hull busied himself between flight missions with a number of Vietnamese children who were always waiting at the outskirts of the base. Several of them had lost arms and legs to the many land mines that were left in the fields or on the roads by retreating battalions or planted by infiltrators. The children seemed to accept their amputations as they accepted the weather. Hull distributed candy to them and talked to them in pidgin American and or in what little Vietnamese he tried his best to learn. When he tried to convince the children in Vietnamese to stay away from cigarettes, they laughed at his pronunciation. Some of the older ones sold marijuana or stronger drugs to the enlisted men and officers on the base. Hull did his best to wean them away from that as well, but the results were minimal. It was not out of moral indignation that he did this. He just resented the use of children in the whole dirty business. When some of the boys tried to interest Hull in their "sisters," he just ignored them. Finally, they learned not to bring up the subject with him. He took some less than humorous barbs from his fellow pilots because of his "code."

"We'll take care of their sisters, Hull. We're good at that," one of them told him mockingly once just before a mission.

Another said, "Hey, Reverend Hull, you're screwing things up for the rest of us."

What made Hull less and less sensitive to the jibes was that in time the children came to like him. They waited for him. They trusted him. And the feeling was reciprocal. He needed them as much as they needed him. When he taught them to play baseball or how to count by fives, it made him forget for an hour or so the strafer and defoliator and firebomber that he became every time he set out on a mission.

The need to stay in touch with children remained with him after he left Vietnam and returned to his home in Chicago. For a while he attempted to find work as a camp counselor or administrator, but he lacked the educational and state certifications. He also suspected that some private institutions refused to hire him because of his appearance. The eyes of the interviewers shifted almost immediately to his missing eyebrows and eyelashes. Nor did he have a hair on his scalp. In response to their unasked questions about how he looked, he explained that he simply lost all the hair on his body after completing his tour in Vietnam.

One day when he read about an opening for a village elementary school teacher in Megiddo, he applied to the sponsoring missionary organization and was immediately hired.

He took a cram course in the language of the country and became fluent quicker than he expected. When he finally settled in Megiddo, he adjusted easily to the pace of village life, liked the children in his charge and kept up his lifelong interest in flying by hang gliding from the cliffs above Megiddo to the valley below. Within a few months he earned the trust of all the people, and he came to be invited occasionally to their houses for a meal or to share in their religious feasts. Some hair began to grow in again but only sparsely, so for the sake of aesthetics he shaved his entire scalp when he shaved the sparse hairs on his face.

The first signs of dizziness and nausea occurred at about this time, but he attributed it a change in climate and diet. When these symptoms persisted, he traveled to the capital to see a doctor, who conducted a series of tests but discovered nothing. The doctor prescribed a special diet and told him his symptoms would probably disappear. And they did. But only for a time.

As each day passed, the raw scars of his memories of Vietnam began to fade. He willed himself to focus only on what he had come to Megiddo to do. True, he could not help but know that various guerrilla groups began their forays against Caseres' territories from staging areas near Megiddo, but he forced himself to think that this was none of his business. He lived day to day. One morning a letter arrived from the doctor he consulted in the capital to inform him that a reevaluation of his tests had come up with a discrepancy. He returned to the capital for additional tests. Finally the doctor informed him that he had a rare type of cancer, probably caused by contact with the various defoliants and sprays that he had spread over the Vietnamese jungles. When Hull asked the doctor if the cancer was treatable, the doctor simply shrugged.

Hull returned to the capital one day before the artillery barrage destroyed the schoolhouse, killing every one of the children who were in it at the time. He and the other villagers recovered body after body from the rubble. When it came time to bury them, the sight of the small bodies cramped into a mass grave was enough to lance open all of Hull's old scars. He felt his warrior blood start to take command of him, and he let it happen. When he heard that a small group of volunteers were going to defend Megiddo against a rumored attack, he knew instantly that he would be one of the volunteers. Somehow he felt that the choice had already been made for him, that he was simply acceding to long-standing orders that had been issued even before he was born. He could not refuse them if he chose.

19

CASERES' DEPARTURE from Magdalena's apartment is the exact replica of his entrance in reverse. The closing of the door, the pause on the small balcony, the eight footsteps to ground level, the opening and shutting of the door of the Mercedes, the thrum of the motor after ignition, the pull away. Magdalena listens but is immune to what she is hearing. Too many visits. Too many. She remembers only the first visit vividly. Every visit after that seems to her like one long visit. But the first visit is clear to her in every detail. And everything that led up to it is clearer still . . .

When Magdalena arrived in the capital from Megiddo, she had only enough money for a week of lodging and food. But that made no difference to her. She was determined never to go back. She began to look for work, but by the end of her sixth day in the capital she had been able to find nothing. She made the rounds to restaurant after restaurant, telling each of the owners that she was a good cook, but none of them wanted a woman from a village in the provinces in their kitchens. She applied for work as a domestic, but there were no openings. It was the usual pattern of refusal after refusal for women like herself. The provincial women who did find jobs as cleaning women or laundresses clung to them possessively so that openings were few. Finally, on the seventh day Magdalena happened to be passing near the train depot as a group of tourists were disembarking from one of the incoming trains and preparing to board buses for a tour of the capital. The bus driver, who was from Magdalena's village and recognized her, approached her and asked her if she would sing for the tourists. When she asked why, he told her that the tourists were members of a symphony orchestra from the United States and had asked him about the music of the country. Magdalena shook her head no, but the bus driver followed her, imploring her to do it since there would be tips, and he would divide the tips equally between the two of them. After a pause Magdalena relented and said she would sing one or two songs. She walked nervously to the side of one of the buses and began to sing one of the songs of her village—a song she learned when she was a child. When she finished, many of the musicians on the bus applauded loudly, and some of them threw money through the bus windows. After she sang her second song, the tourists threw her more money. Other people who were waiting at the station formed a circle around her and applauded as well. Just before the bus left the depot, the bus driver bunched several bills and thrust them in Magdalena's hand and told her to come the next day to the same place at the same time. She did. The tourists who heard her sing then tipped her even more generously than did the musicians. Within a week other bus drivers asked her to sing for their groups as well, and by the time a month had passed Magdalena's recitals at the depot were an expected, discussed, and eventually advertised part of every tourist's initiation to the capital. In addition, her fellow countrymen and countrywomen became a part of her growing audience so that she often sang for groups as large as two or three hundred people and had to move from the depot to the plaza to accommodate the crowds.

The reason for her popularity seemed to be that Magdalena sang only the simple, old, and melodic songs that were part of the folklore of the country. They touched not only a nostalgic but spiritual vein in her listeners, many of whom had become bored with the new songs that were nothing but adapted versions of electronic compositions from the United States or else melodramatic, patriotic ballads by the officially approved state composers.

As month succeeded month, Magdalena's name became known to an ever widening audience. The music critic from the country's only newspaper attended one of her recitals and promptly dubbed her "The Dove from the Mountains." By the end of the first year, she was no longer giving recitals but concerts once a week in the capital's main amphitheater. The bus driver from her village became her manager, and he eventually succeeded in negotiating a contract for her to record her songs. Her popularity quickened as a result. By the end of her second year in the capital, the recordings of her weekly concerts sold more and more copies. Part of her popularity had to do with her appearance as well as with her voice. She typified in every way the beauty associated with the women of the country. She was tall, high-breasted, and erect whether standing or walking. Her full, straight black hair framed her face like a cowl, emphasizing her deep-set brown eyes, limpidly long eyelashes, and winglike eyebrows. When she acknowledged applause or praise, she seemed to release a smile that made her admirers feel it was bestowed on them alone.

In the middle of the third year, the number of people at her concerts and the number of those who purchased recordings reached a plateau. Magdalena realized then that her village songs appealed only to a minority of the population, and that the minority had been sated. She then tried to change her style and sang some of the current songs that she previously shunned, but neither her voice nor her manner were suitable to the music. Several months later the producers at the amphitheater began to phase out her concerts from once a week to once a month to none at all. The recording company owners cancelled her contract. After her bus driver-manager returned to his job, Magdalena began singing four nights a week at one of the taverns for sailors at the port. She refused to sing anything but the village songs with which she felt most comfortable. Whenever the sailors disapproved or shouted or whistled or made blatantly provocative or obscene gestures at her, she retained enough of her former sense of presence to keep them in their place. She would simply stop singing in midsong, address them from the stage in her village dialect as if she had a sister's or a mother's right in the matter of their behavior, and the sailors would immediately grow quiet, even sheepish. Then, and only then, would she resume singing.

Even with her diminished income she managed to live better than she could have hoped to live in Megiddo. She continued to make sure that her mother and her brother Joseph were regularly supplied with all the money they required to meet their needs. But during the winter when the ships were fewer and the sailors but a fraction of the number that usually stayed in port, her wages declined. The tavern owner could only afford to hire her for two nights a week, then one, then none.

It was at this time that she first heard from Caseres. One night after she had finished singing at the tavern, the tavern owner told her that a car was waiting for her at the side door. When she went to the door, she was informed politely but explicitly by two men in uniform that the premier wished to see her. She asked why, but the soldiers acted as if she had no right to ask the question. Taking her by either arm, they ushered her into the car. The fact that she was given no choice paralyzed her for a moment, but by the time she recovered her courage the car was in motion with the uniformed men seated on each side of her.

When they finally reached the official residence of the premier, the soldiers escorted Magdalena to an anteroom and told her to wait. An hour passed before a door at the opposite end of the anteroom opened, and she was suddenly facing a tall, spear-straight man whom she immediately recognized as Caseres himself. He wore a tan shirt open at the collar and riding breeches and brown boots. He paced the room for several minutes before he walked toward her. Then he sat beside her and studied her for a moment that she thought longer than necessary.

"So," he said finally, "you are Magdalena . . . *the* Magdalena."

"Yes, Excellency."

Magdalena tried to appear relaxed, but she felt her lower lip quiver until she had to bite it to stop it. She had heard many stories about Caseres and how he often summoned women who provoked his fancy. The women would be confronted by uniformed men and told that the premier was interested in seeing them. If they demurred, the soldiers would "conduct" them in much the same way in which Magdalena herself had been "conducted" earlier in the evening. Some of the summoned women never revealed what had happened to them. Others did and told how they had been abused or threatened by implied or direct threats to their lives or to the lives of members of their families. All the abuses were sexual. Apparently the premier summoned any woman who happened to intrigue or arouse him, and the list of those summoned included maids as well as dowagers, actresses and the wives of government officials. One waitress related how she was brought to the premier's office and how he simply forced her down on the rug in front of his desk without so much as saying a word to her. When he had finished with her, he stood, rebuttoned his trousers and returned to his chair behind the desk where he continued to work with papers that her "visit" had momentarily interrupted.

Magdalena knew some of these abused women personally since they worked near the tavern at the port. Their fear of the premier was genuine. A few of the women revealed how their husbands had abandoned them once they knew that their wives had become identified among the premier's "sows." Most of the women feared being summoned again even though Caseres was never known to repeat himself.

"How long have you been singing?" Caseres asked Magdalena.

"A little more than two years in the capital."

"Sing for me."

"Pardon me, Excellency?"

"Sing for me. Sing a song for me here. Now." He paused and studied her face. "Do you know the song about the sailor and the mermaid?"

"Yes, Excellency."

"Sing it for me then. It's been a long time since I heard it."

After a pause Magdalena sang all seven verses of the song while Caseres remained seated beside her and listened without taking his eyes off her for a second.

"That was beautiful," he said when she finished. He smiled and applauded.

"Thank you, Excellency."

Caseres put his hand on Magdelana's shoulder, and she felt herself trembling in spite of herself.

"Are you afraid of me?" asked Caseres.

"Yes, Excellency. I am."

"Don't be. You're not the same as the others." He removed his hand and made a gesture with it as if he were addressing a crowd. "You have the old spirit that we need in this country."

Not knowing how to answer or if she should, Magdalena remained silent.

"Very well, you may leave now," said Caseres, standing. "I'll have the men who brought you take you home." He removed an envelope from his pocket and handed it to her. "Take it. Open it."

Magdalena reached into the envelope and removed a pack of newly minted bills.

"I am embarrassed to accept this, Excellency," said Magdalena, returning the bills to the envelope.

"Don't be embarrassed," said Caseres, taking a step or two away from her. "You've been taking bills like this for some time now. I've been doing it through the tavern-keeper. I told him to pretend it was your wages." He waited to see if she was making the connection, and she was. "But I think it's time to do away with that. Now I am doing it directly so you can dispense with your appearances at the tavern. I don't like to think of you in those surroundings. Pearls before swine."

Magdalena sat without speaking while Caseres called an order in the direction of the room where the two soldiers who had brought Magdalena to the residence were waiting.

"These men will take you back," he said.

After Magdalena stood and headed for the door, she stopped and asked hesitantly, "Why are you doing this for me, Excellency?"

"Why? It is my pleasure. I like your songs. I like the way you sing them." He paused and faced her directly while the soldiers watched him from the doorway. "Relax, Magdalena. I could have had you brought here months ago if I wanted it that way. I didn't have to wait until now when you've become, shall we say, less popular. I've followed your career very closely. I know that you really have no place to go now but back to your village. I don't think you want to do that. So just take the money and use it any way you choose. That way you can stay here as long as you want. There will be more envelopes coming. Regularly."

Every week after that an envelope containing the same amount of newly minted currency was delivered in person to Magdalena by one of Caseres' personal guards. Within weeks, word of Caseres' patronage of Magdalena reached the tavern keeper. Anxious to exploit the fact that Magdalena was now sponsored by Caseres, he invited Magdalena to sing regularly at the tavern. Magdalena declined. It was at that moment that she faced her alternatives, and they were exactly what Caseres told her they were. One option was to return to the village, and the other was to remain in the capital by continuing to accept the weekly envelopes from Caseres. The thought of returning home repelled her. After having lived in the capital, the village presented itself as a primitive alternative. It made her feel that she was confronting death itself. On the other hand, she knew that continuing to accept the weekly envelopes from Caseres was bound to leave her indebted to him even though she did not know how. For weeks she debated what to do. During that time the envelopes arrived with their usual punctuality, and she accepted each of them. Little by little, perhaps through gossip spread by the tavern keeper, it became common knowledge that Magdalena had a special relationship with the premier. Instead of being an onus, it became a bonus. Her former recording company invited her to return and record new songs for distribution. When she agreed to do it, she sensed a new hospitality where before there had only been dismissal. She began to be treated with more than usual deference. She found herself gradually recovering the reputation she thought she had lost forever, and in a matter of a few months she regained her former status almost completely.

The envelopes continued to be delivered at the same intervals. Finally, one evening when she was alone in her apartment, Caseres himself was the messenger. He stood in the doorway, envelope visibly in hand. Magdalena, having become so accustomed to the weekly deliveries by others, had almost forgotten that Caseres was the real disburser. She faced him with a mixture of surprise and fear. He walked past her, dropped the envelope on her coffee table and seated himself with a soft grunt in a reading chair she kept near the window. For several minutes Magdalena watched him while he rubbed his eyes with the knuckles of both hands and then clasped his hands behind his neck and stared at her.

"You look as if I had to have your permission to come here," he said with a smile.

Magdalena did not move. Caseres rose from the chair and strode toward her. She could smell rum on his breath.

"I don't bother with permission, Magdalena," he said and put his hand directly on her right breast and then slowly withdrew it.

She backed away reflexively from his touch and said, "Is this the reason you were sending the envelopes to me?" She put her hand on her breast where he had touched her.

"Do you want me to answer that?"

"Yes," she said. After a pause she added softly, "No."

"The money was nothing, Magdalena. I don't need to buy people. Nothing is forbidden for me. All I have to do is give an order. But you? You were a special case."

"Why?"

"I have my reasons." He looked directly into her eyes. "But remember, you didn't have to accept the envelopes. You could have gone back to your family. No one was stopping you."

She turned her face away from him, but he took her chin gently with one hand and made her look at him . . .

Later she would ask herself why she surrendered to him without another word, why she let him fondle her there in the middle of the room before they went together into her bedroom, why she continued to lie nude on her bed afterward and watch him with a feeling of both disgust and, curiously, admiration as he dressed and left her, why she subsequently resigned herself to his periodic and unannounced visits and why she even began to look forward to them, why she gradually grew into the role of his lover without feeling any hesitancy or doubt about it at all. In a matter of a few months, her life with Caseres became her private domain, not to be shared with anyone else but him. He showed her a side of himself she never believed existed or could exist. He dropped his public face and began to confide in her. Frequently his visits would end without any physical intimacy between them. On several occasions he would come and sit in the chair by the window and then leave without saying a word.

After his heart attack, Caseres did not see her or communicate with her for months. Finally, he arrived one evening, again without warning. He spoke as if nothing had happened. It was as if he had seen her only days before. She noticed that he was slightly thinner. He showed her a small packet that he kept in his tunic pocket. He said it contained glycerin tablets. Thereafter whenever his breathing became labored or whenever he put his hand on his sternum as if he were experiencing a hint of pain or constriction there, he would remove the packet, place a glycerin tablet under his tongue and resume what he had been saying or doing.

His sexual interest in Magdalena intensified rather than weakened as a result of his heart attack. Once, while they were lying side by side after intercourse, he whispered to her that the "time bomb" in his chest made his pleasure with her even keener because he looked on each of his visits as his last. His condition limited his abilities as a lover, and more than once he let Magdalena pleasure him in a variety of ways that made little demand on him physically. Sensing his anxiety, she tried to insure that his climaxes were fairly rapid so that he would not be taxed unnecessarily by any progression of excitement. Nevertheless, Caseres always kept the glycerin tablets within reach, and it was not infrequent for him to slip a tablet into his mouth before he made love to her or she, him.

20

KRONOS SWEARS TO HIMSELF that this will be his last battle. He assumes that his age and time in service must be responsible for his attitude. When he was a young soldier, he could not wait for the attack orders to be given. Once, after an attack had begun and the battle joined, he had gone without sleep for more than forty hours without having any sense of fatigue. On the contrary, he felt exhilarated, and the exhilaration of the fight kept him not only awake but alert. It was at such moments that he was at his best. His superior officers made note of the fact that he took risks with his life under fire. Their high regard for his seemingly reckless courage in battle earned Kronos a lieutenancy, and his ascent in the ranks continued after that.

Remembering his younger self, Kronos feels the familiar exhilaration for the battle of Megiddo try to possess him like the first wave of desire for a woman, but the deliciousness of it is soon thinned and counterbalanced by what he knows will happen when the shooting starts. It is this growing awareness of the possibilities—not of death but of pain—that has gradually gotten the better of him. Where had he read that men fear torture more than death, which he translated to mean that men fear suffering more than death? For Kronos, death never presented itself as other than a void. Each time he had had to face it in combat, he tried to face it as if it were just another enemy, but he always came away with the realization that there was nothing really to face.

It is the chance of being wounded or maimed that eats at him now like a cancer, and he has seen enough wounds to know that death is certainly not the worst thing that can happen to a man. The images of armless, legless, and chinless soldiers rush through his memory like a gallery of the grotesque, and he slouches against his backpack, knowing all at once what it must mean to be a hundred and fifty years old.

When he lifts his head and surveys the soldiers in bivouac around him, he sees them suddenly as if they were sleeping moles or young rabbits in a warren. They shelter themselves as well as they can against the chill of the valley night, cringing under their ponchos or else curled in their foxholes in the sleep of snails. Kronos for a moment imagines that everyone and everything around him is under the command of fear. It is not merely the fear of the unknown that he tastes now at the back of his tongue like curdled milk. It is the fear that all soldiers feel when they know they might be killed in multiple ways and when this makes them realize that they will become the killers of others. It is the same fear that will make them crouch, not stand, when they try to avoid strafing fire as they weave their way up the slopes to Megiddo.

Yes, mutters Kronos to himself, this will be his last battle. He's had enough of tactics, enough of living with losses. He hopes that the reconnaissance of Megiddo is correct and that dawn will present him and his men with an abandoned village, nothing more. Above all, he does not want a repetition of the skirmish that happened in the village of Paz ten weeks before. Caseres had ordered that Paz should be taken because it had become, like Megiddo, a staging area for raids into the interior. Kronos had prepared his men for the attack with his customary care. First, there had been the usual reconnaissance by scouting parties on foot. Then the attack began. Kronos remained with the rear guard until his forward platoons occupied Paz without resistance. Later his lieutenants reported to Kronos that the soldiers had entered house after house, pulling women and children into the square where they bayoneted them all to death. The final toll was well over one hundred. Only a few of the village men were included in the count since most of them had gone into the capital to trade their produce for foodstuffs, cloth, and other supplies. Kronos learned that the soldiers were not satisfied only with bayoneting their victims. They began scavenging for rings, bracelets, and even gold teeth. They sliced off fingers, arms, and cheeks to get them. By the time Kronos arrived in Paz, he was appalled by the slaughter, but it was too late to do anything except excoriate officers and soldiers alike, then order them out of the village and back to the capital. For the entire summer after the attack, the name of the village of Paz appeared in newspapers throughout the world. Caseres was berated by the Americans for having ordered the attack in the first place, and they threatened him with a cutoff of all further foreign aid and ordnance. His only reply to the Americans was to stress that the attack was a matter of self-defense, to which every nation was entitled, and that it would have a purifying effect on an otherwise troublesome part of the border.

Six months after the attack, one of Kronos' lieutenants was kidnapped. Nothing was heard from the kidnappers for more than a week. Then the first box arrived at Kronos' headquarters. It was the size of a hatbox, and it contained the lieutenant's head. Other boxes arrived after that, each containing a part of the lieutenant's body.

21

THE CORSICAN FEELS SOMETHING between sympathy and concern for Joseph, as if he were, not his father, but an uncle. He asks himself why he permitted the boy to become involved in this. Then he remembers how adamant Joseph had been, how difficult he had been to dissuade, how the boy persisted until there was nothing left to do but let him come along.

"I want you to promise me something, Joseph," says the Corsican.

"Yes, sir."

"Tomorrow I want you to promise me that you will not take any foolish chances."

"I will not do anything foolish, sir. I asked to come here to be a fighter. I want to be here."

"That's not what I mean. I mean I want you to come out of this alive. If you listen to me, you will. I want this to be your first and last battle. Promise me that you will listen to everything I tell you to do."

Joseph looks at him with surprise.

"Do you promise me?" repeats the Corsican.

"If you want me to promise, I promise, sir."

"Do you mean it?"

Joseph looks at the ground. "I don't know, sir."

The Corsican breaks off and looks away. He is wondering what he expected the boy to say.

"Sir?" asks Joseph, breaking the silence.

"Yes."

"Tomorrow will be my last battle, sir."

"Good."

"I am not thinking about any others after tomorrow. Just tomorrow."

22

WHILE SABERTES WAITS in his foxhole for Hull so that they can go together to meet with the Corsican, he removes a leather-bound notebook the size of a breviary from his shirt pocket. He flips through it quickly, noting that every page is now filled with his handwriting. As has become his habit, he turns to the first page and begins reading. The entries are all in chronological order, and he knows he will not stop reading until he reaches the end.

Today I left my parish to join the resistance against Caseres. Perhaps, like our Lord, I will now begin the Passion of Julio Sabertes. It is the appropriate week for it. All I know is that I cannot serve simply as a minister of the sacraments any longer. The oppression by Caseres continues. I cannot go on like some Pharisee, pretending that nothing is happening. I know what is happening. I see it every day. I must dedicate myself to a new priesthood where I not only pray for the end of this evil, but I work against it by fighting it. May God be with me . . .

This is my first day with the cadre. They accept me as I am, and I am known to them simply as Sabertes, which is what I prefer. Tomorrow morning I will join the unit being trained in the tactics of guerrilla warfare. The textbook is by Mao. There is no uniform, but somehow all of us look alike in our different clothes. I have decided not to celebrate Holy Mass as long as I am with the cadre. I will dedicate my resistance to Caseres as my Mass . . .

Just another day with the guerrilla platoon. As a matter of fact no one asks about the date or even what day it is. Today I was issued an automatic rifle. It was manufactured somewhere in Czechoslovakia. It took me several hours to wipe the cosmoline and grease from the barrel and chamber. Afterward I had to swab the bore until it glistened. Then I was taught how to load and unload it . . .

On the rifle range I fired a dozen or so rounds. The recoil of the weapon startled me. I only pray that I never will have to aim at another human being and have to shoot him. But if I must, I will do it. Why else did I come here? But in my heart I feel that I can never do it. I know what a bullet can do to a body. Tomorrow there is a raid in the offing. I have been told that I will go as an observer only, not a fighter. I had not expected to see action so soon. But I pray I am ready . . .

When I joined the group that was going to raid the forwarding depot near Virgo del Mar, I met with Omar. He is from my home village. He was glad to see me, but it was difficult to relax with him because we both knew what was ahead of us. He had been on several raids already. He looked pale. Once we were on the move, he told me that he was still suffering from dysentery. To build up his strength, he said that he had been eating oranges and bananas and grapefruit. He warned me to be extremely careful of the water I drank. Or of anything washed in the same water . . .

Back in camp now after the raid, which turned out not to be a raid at all. We were in the jungle for three days. We never reached the supply depot. The jungle had grown so thick after the rains that our machetes could not hack a path through it. We would cut and hack for four or five hours and move ahead less than thirty yards. Finally, on Thursday the commander of the platoon accepted the inevitable and cancelled the mission. The mosquitoes and leeches were a constant problem. We had to stretch our ponchos in the trees to be free of leeches. Omar had a difficult time of it. From time to time he would disappear into the bush and relieve himself, and we could hear him moaning or retching. But each time he returned and refused any special attention. It is amazing what some men are able to endure when their purpose in living is more than a concern for their own lives . . .

When we made our way back into camp, Omar collapsed. After he regained consciousness, he still refused any help for himself. He just went to his cot like a wounded animal and dealt with his pain by himself. This impresses me more than I can say . . .

This afternoon a small plane passed over us. Of course, our camp is not visible from the air, but none of us doubted that those in the plane knew we were in the area. They dropped pamphlets which advised us to surrender, to place our trust in the government, to avail ourselves of a general amnesty. None of the men even bothered to look up at the plane. When the pamphlets finally settled, they remained where they landed. A few of the men gathered some of them for toilet paper. Omar seemed much improved. We talked for some time, and I told him what I knew about his family and friends at home. He savored every word as if I were placing the host in his mouth . . .

Today I was taught two things. The first was how to defend myself if I were without a weapon and were suddenly attacked. The instructor told us to pretend that the only thing we had to protect ourselves was a newspaper. He said we could assume that the attack was coming and that we had time to roll up the newspaper tightly so that it had the shape and thickness of a nightstick or a baton. Then we were told to grab it not at the ends but in the middle and hold it that way. If we held it that way, we could strike the attacker as he approached. We could bring the baton from below and up so that it would catch him in the groin or under the chin or the nose. I could not understand how this was possible until I rolled the newspaper up myself the way he described. Holding it in the middle, I felt that it had the stiffness of a piece of wood, which shouldn't have surprised me since paper comes from wood pulp anyway. The second thing I learned was that the initiative in any battle is always with the attacker. In urban warfare this is particularly true. For example, to bring all the work in a major build-ing to a complete standstill, all that is necessary is to call the operator at the switchboard and tell her that a bomb has been placed in the building and has been set to detonate at such-and-such an hour. The result will be the complete evacuation of the building and then the slow office-by-office search for the explosive. Regular work will be totally disrupted. And all of this could be provoked by a single telephone call. Multiply this tactic by hundreds of calls, and it is easy to understand how an entire city could be paralyzed. To make the tactic viable, we were told that an actual bomb should be placed at some point, but in fact the very threat of a bomb would be enough to bring life to a halt . . .

This morning the briefing centered on the importance of guerrilla groups to stay "underground." That way their very "invisibility" makes them more dangerous than they actually may be. As long as they maintain their invisibility, they can go on functioning and retain their initiative as attackers. What often happens to guerrilla groups, we were told, is that their very success breeds an arrogance of power, and they begin to be more visible so that they can receive public glory for their successes. This inclination to want to take credit is their worst enemy. Once out in the open, they are seen for what they actually are. The mystery is gone, and with it goes the power that mystery creates. From that point on it is only a matter of time before they are defeated. We were told that the success of the Mafia in the United States was always based on the fact the leaders of the various families always denied that the Mafia existed. I discovered that the word itself comes from Arabic. It means "there is nothing . . . "

We are scheduled for an attack tomorrow . . .

After the attack on the base, we were all captured. I am writing this a month later. The militia was prepared for us. Someone must have informed them in advance. After they kept us in separate cells for two days, we were all taken into a large warehouse where the officer in command asked which one of us was a priest. No one looked at me, and I kept looking straight ahead. The officer ordered us back into our cells. The next day we were taken to the warehouse again, but some of the men were missing who had been with us the first time. The officer explained with a trace of a smile that they had gone to "paradise." He asked again if there was a priest among us and that it would be wise if the priest stepped forward voluntarily. Still no one looked at me.

There were two women in our group, and the officer had his soldiers pull them out of line. Then he ordered the soldiers to strip them of their clothes, and the officer kept his eyes on the rest of us while the soldiers did unspeakable things to the women. They tried to make the women do things to one another, but they refused. Finally, they brought dogs, and the soldiers held the women while the officer tried to get the dogs to mount them. Two of the men beside me broke from their positions and rushed toward the women to help them, but the officer fired two shots from his pistol, and both men fell before they had taken six steps. When the officer saw that one of the men was still alive, he simply walked toward him and administered a coup de grace.

Only five of us were left in line. After we watched the soldiers drag the women away, we were left standing while the officer paced back and forth in front of us. From time to time he would stop, and each time he stopped he lifted his pistol and aimed it at the men who happened to be in front of him. As soon as a man broke from the line and made a dash for the fence, the officer shot him. The tension of not knowing what was going to happen while we waited in line became unbearable. One by one the other three men broke away from the line and tried to reach the fence, and the officer shot them all. Finally I was the only one left standing. The officer approached me and smiled. He addressed me as "Father." Then he said I should have stepped forward in the beginning, and that would have saved all the ones who were now dead. He said he knew I was a priest because of the expression on my face. He said I had the look of a man who had already accepted his death. I said nothing. Then he told me that all the others had died because of me, and that the women would die as well since they were no longer any good for anything. He said that I would be released because, since I was responsible for the deaths of all my comrades, it would take me longer to die if I lived on, knowing that.

23

TWO FARMERS LIFT THE BOY Radames had struck with his Porsche. A third man holds the boy's broken and bleeding left leg. Trying to be gentle while simultaneously coordinating their steps, the men sidle up the berm, cross the highway and inch their way with extra care down the slope of the opposite berm. They head toward a village that is approximately a hundred yards away. Some of the crowd that gathered on the highway after the accident follow the men toward the village while the rest, after first noticing and then skirting the run-over white dog, return to whatever they were doing before the accident happened.

The old man who had been on the donkey that the boy was leading is still walking back and forth on the shoulder of the highway. With every step he makes a pleading gesture toward the sky like a pilgrim desperately invoking the help of God. Pressing his hands to his temples, he begins to wail. Meanwhile the donkey is munching grass beside the dead dog. At last the old man seizes the donkey's tether and leads him after the small group already heading in the direction of the village.

Once they reach the village, the farmers carry the boy into the first house they pass and lay him carefully on the dirt floor. When they cut his trousers from his left leg, they look but say nothing. The boy, pale from shock and loss of blood, is awake now, and he keeps asking about his dog, about the old man and the donkey, about his dog again and again. The men nod but do not answer.

Looking at the exposed leg, which is angled unnaturally awry at the knee, the men shake their heads in unison as if there is nothing more that they can do. A broken bone above the knee has burst through the skin, and the jagged, bloody edges of the bone have small bits of leg flesh on them. Two women have entered the house in the meanwhile. They approach the men, exchange a few words and almost reverently move toward the boy and begin to attend to him. The men leave.

Still shaking their heads and whispering to one another, both farmers watch the old man as he leads the donkey toward them. The old man is still whimpering. He seems totally bewildered. The men ask him to tell them what happened, and the old man relates, with gestures, what he remembers. As he concludes, he mentions that the car was white.

"Small car?" asks one of the men. He kneels on one knee and draws an outline of a coupe on the ground.

The old man nods a definite yes.

"Radames," says the man, rising and wiping the outline of the coupe away with his heel. "He drives to his villa on this road. He is the only one with a car like that. I've seen him many times."

Just as he finishes speaking, his companion points toward the road. A white Porsche hurtles by in the direction of the capital. Radames in full uniform is at the wheel. He passes the spot of the accident without glancing right or left or bothering to slacken his speed. The old man looks where the man is pointing just in time to glimpse the car. For an instant he seems to lose his mind. He jumps up and down, pulling at his clothes and pointing at the car.

The third man, the one who was holding the boy's leg when he was carried to the village, finally leads the old man into the house and makes him sit down. The old man is weeping now but without a sound.

Outside the house the two farmers are still talking.

"You were r-r-r-right," says one. "It was R-R-R-Radames."

"I knew it."

"What is there to d–d–d–do?"

"If he has gone to the capital, then later he must return to the villa." He looks directly into his companion's eyes. "This time we will be waiting for him."

24

"THERE IS NOTHING TO BE WORRIED ABOUT, Ambassador Nesbitt," says Caseres, rising from his chair and walking slowly to the window.

"Let's hope so." Ambassador Nesbitt is well over six feet tall with grayish-white hair parted on the left side. He wears a tan tropical suit, a white shirt, and a plain maroon necktie. His glasses have black frames and contradict the color scheme of his clothes.

"This village has been a problem to me for more than five years," Caseres continues. "If I leave it there, it will fill again with pus like a boil. It's time to lance it, to break the houses down to stone, to make it a symbol."

"My government has no quibble with you for what you've done internally up to now. Artillery barrages, even if they're near the border, can always be chalked up to self-defense or ridding the country of infiltrators. But hot pursuit with a full battalion that may spill over the border is something else, and there's a rumor that you might even use air . . . "

"How did you learn we would be using a full battalion?"

"Let's just say that we have ways."

"Are you bribing my officers?"

"That's privileged information. But let's not get into that. Whether you use a battalion or your whole army, the important thing is that this raid gets no publicity whatsoever. Your soldiers must do the job and get out fast. But no air can be used. And the whole operation must receive no report at all, especially in the foreign press. Can you guarantee that there will be no press?"

"That's already been taken care of, Mr. Ambassador. We have, to use your language, our ways as well. "

"Then you'll have no problem with this American. And if you have no problem with me, you'll have no problem with my government." He pauses, removes his glasses, and massages his forehead as if to ease a migraine. "The arms and supplies that were given to you by Washington are for self-defense only. If it ever gets back that you're using these weapons to wipe out a village or chase guerrillas across the border into another sovereignty, then the whole program of military aid will be stopped. Some of our congressmen and senators have gotten very hard-headed since Vietnam. They know that their voters don't want any more snafus . . . "

"What is that word?"

"Snafus?" says Ambassador Nesbitt. "It's American slang. It means mistakes. They don't want any more expensive mistakes. If it means writing you off so they can stay in office, believe me when I tell you that the politicians will write you off. And that includes the president."

"There will be no writing off, Mr. Ambassador."

Both Caseres and Nesbitt turn when they hear a knock at the office door. Nesbitt looks at the door and then at Caseres as if he is waiting for an answer to an unasked question, but Caseres in response crosses purposefully to the door and opens it. Standing there in uniform is Radames.

"Come in, Radames," says Caseres, closing the door behind him as he follows Radames into the room. "Radames, this is Ambassador Nesbitt from the American Embassy."

Radames bows toward Nesbitt, and Nesbitt nods his head as an acknowledgment.

"I've asked my son to join us, Mr. Ambassador," says Caseres. "I hope you don't mind, but I want him to know the significance of the celebration in the stadium. He will reap the benefits in time so it is important for him to be here today. I want your president to know that there will be continuity, genuine continuity."

"Your father has been a good ally of the United States in this part of the world," says Nesbitt to Radames.

Radames sits down with obvious discomfort between his father and the ambassador. It's quite apparent that his uniform is too small for him, binding him across the shoulders and in the crotch. Noticing this, Caseres tells him with a smile that he is beginning to "outgrow" his clothes.

Ambassador Nesbitt is saying, "I will have everybody from the embassy in attendance at the stadium, and I have a special proclamation from the president himself that is being translated as we speak so that it will be able to be read aloud at the ceremony."

"That's very kind of you. Please convey my thanks to the president."

"It's the least we can do for a dependable ally," says Nesbitt. "And I think it's safe to say that the relationship between your country and the United States of America can continue as long as there are no, shall we say, problems."

"There will be no problems," says Caseres and draws his chair closer to Nesbitt. "I think it is advisable that we should discuss the implications of the celebration today so that we have a common understanding. You probably know that I have developed some medical problems lately."

Nesbitt nods.

"Because of that," Caseres resumes, "I want to make sure that my son Radames will receive the same cooperation that I've enjoyed for many years now with the United States, no matter which party was in power." He pauses. "I would not like to see the work of a lifetime vanish because we did not make sufficient preparations and did not understand one another completely."

"As a father myself, I think I can understand that."

"This goes beyond fatherhood, Mr. Ambassador. It involves the future of the country itself. As long as I'm in power, the country will stay as you see it. But should something happen to me . . . "

"Because of the medical condition you mentioned?"

"Precisely." He pauses, turning first to Radames and then back to Nesbitt. "I need your assurance that your policies in this part of the world will not change."

Nesbitt stands and extends his hand. Caseres take it, and both men shake hands.

"You have my word that nothing will change," says Nesbitt in the tone of a pledge.

25

FOR NESBITT, dealing with Caseres was not unlike dealing with the Mafia. As long as points of mutual interest were agreed upon and met, there was no problem. You could bank on the pact that was struck, and there would be no deviations. He had had enough experience with such dealings in his various businesses before he was named to an ambassadorship.

Once when the workers at one of his plants were threatening to strike, Nesbitt had a meeting with the leadership. During the meeting, it became apparent to Nesbitt that the leadership would be willing to head off the strike if certain personal financial conditions were met . . . their *own* personal financial conditions. No document was ever signed, and the exact terms were never specified, but every month Nesbitt made sure that a considerable sum of money was delivered in cash to the leadership. There was no strike. When some of the workers continued to demonstrate, the leadership saw to it that they were properly "disciplined."

Running seven plants in different parts of the country and one in Honduras did not provide Nesbitt with the drama he needed in his life. The world of business intrigued him in the beginning, but once he mastered the basics and saw that his only reward was more and more money, he became not so much tired of it as bored. He began to invest in works of art. His accountant told him that such "collectibles" were a good investment in the "long run," and he listened. Since he knew next to nothing about art, he found little to enjoy in the paintings beyond the pleasure of knowing he owned them. The only drama for him came in the acquisition, and there it was just a matter of outbidding an opponent. The tactics were the same as they were in business, and he soon tired of that as well. Then several of his friends tried to interest him in part ownership of a baseball team. But when the politics of the owners came in conflict with the enthusiasm of some of the local boosters and politicians, he decided that this was a headache he could do without.

One night when he and his wife were driving home from a visit with their eldest son and his family, he was surprised to hear his wife suggest, "Why don't you get interested in politics yourself?"

"What kind of politics?"

"Politics. Party politics."

"That's not for me. I contribute to the party. Every time they need something, they know where to find me."

"But you don't follow up. I'll bet you've given a small fortune to local and state and even national candidates, but you never collect. You never ask them to return the favor."

"I don't need them. As long as the right party wins, that's all I'm concerned about."

"But why don't you focus on giving just to the biggies? You know—presidential candidates, vice presidential candidates. If they're elected, they have plums to give away. You never know what they might offer you."

"There's a limit on what you can give now."

"I don't mean just money. Make a gift of one of your paintings to some front-runner. Host a dinner. Have a money-raiser. One thousand dollars a plate, that kind of thing. There are a lot of people you know who would shell out more than that if you invited them to something you sponsored. Or else let one of the leading candidates use our place in Jamaica for a little rest and relaxation. Even if they refuse, they'll remember your name."

"What about the business?"

"Ned can run the business. He's old enough now. And you've already taught him everything that a father can teach a son." She paused to let her suggestions sink in. "It's just something to think about."

And he did think about it. In order to keep his options open, he thought it best to contribute equally to both parties. When asked why, he answered with a straight face that he believed in the two-party system and wanted to make sure it stayed healthy. For two successive years after that, he was photographed with several presidential aspirants during the opening round of a golf tournament he underwrote. He made sure that the right number of Hollywood actors and actresses were present at the dinner following the tournament so as to guarantee newspaper and television interest. And he remembered these same aspirants on their birthdays by sending them fourteen-karat miniature putters with their names engraved on the putting blades. Because of all these efforts, Nesbitt and his wife began to be included on the dinner lists of the governor and the state senators. On two occasions subsequently they were guests of the president at the White House.

"If he runs again and wins, I think he'll offer you an ambassadorship," Nesbitt's wife told him at the conclusion of their second visit.

"So I've heard."

"Do they give you a choice of countries when they appoint you like that?"

"I don't know. Sometimes they prefer career diplomats, sometimes not. All I know is that we could supplement our entertainment budgets as Mr. and Mrs. Ambassador a lot easier than some career diplomats could."

"I'd feel a lot better if you knew another language."

"That's not decisive. Everybody understands English these days."

"I hope we get something somewhere in Europe. I'll spend all my time shopping in antique shops."

"All Europe is an antique shop."

When Nesbitt learned later that the ambassadorship that was offered him was not in Europe, he thought first of turning it down. But again his wife intervened.

"If you do a good job where they want you now, they'll offer you something better later. I've talked to a lot of women in Washington, and they tell me that's how the system works."

Their first year at their post was different enough from their American way of life to give them a sense of novelty and adventure. They had all the domestic help they needed. Nesbitt's wife busied herself with refurnishing and redecorating the embassy. That took almost a year, but at the end of the year she began looking around nervously for something "creative" to do. At the end of the second year, she stayed less and less in the country and more and more in their home in the United States or their estate in Jamaica. When she returned to the official residence adjacent to the embassy, she was constantly battling with the staff, finding fault with the meals, the gardens, the way the chauffeur drove, the weather, and, at last, the country itself.

"If we stay here another year," she said one morning to Nesbitt at breakfast, "I'll go out of my mind."

"Just remember that this was your idea in the beginning, Nell," said Nesbitt.

"So what? Why do you have to listen to everything I suggest? Don't you have a mind of your own? I was only making a suggestion. I'm not an expert on these subjects."

As the months passed, he noticed that she was beginning to drink earlier and earlier during the day. Without telling her, he wrote to the appropriate officials in Washington, inquiring about a change of assignment. He specifically mentioned a country in Europe that he knew his wife preferred. The response was that the president thought he was doing a superior job where he was and that he had no one else in the wings who could work with Caseres as well as he could.

The more he thought about it, the more the years of running his own business filled him with a desire to return to the life he left. As a business leader, he made all the important decisions. He took orders from no one. As an ambassador, he was no longer in charge. He had to report. He had to wait for instructions. He asked himself again and again why he had gotten himself into this position in the first place.

26

THE ONLY LIGHT in the Corsican's bunker comes from a flashlight propped against a rock on the floor so that the yellow
beam vees outward to illuminate a map of the village that he
has drawn on the dirt floor with his knife. The Corsican sits
behind the flashlight, and Hull and Sabertes squat on the flanks
of the triangle cast by its beam.

"You both know that there are only two entries to Megiddo,"
says the Corsican. He lifts his knife and jabs the point at two
places on the dirt map. "One is here, and the other is here. The
artillery bombardment left the wall between those two points
intact. I've checked it myself. There are no gaps anywhere.
This means that the two original gates are the only ways in and
out of Megiddo." He looks questioningly at Hull and Sabertes
to make sure they understand the implications of his statement.
Then he gazes up at a man who is standing behind Sabertes.
The man has a full black beard, but it has the look of having
been trimmed. He is wearing what appear to be army fatigues.
He has an automatic weapon slung over his right shoulders,
and he is smoking a slim cigar slowly, as if he is thinking while
he smokes.

"Lubo," the Corsican says to the man, "what this means is
that you and your men in the mountains must wait and hold your
fire until the soldiers start to retreat through the gates and down
the slopes . . . "

"*If* there is a retreat," says Lubo, flicking the ashes from his cigar on the map.

"There will be a retreat. Leave that to us," he states and pauses. "We will let the soldiers enter Megiddo through the two gates. We will let as many as possible enter before we begin firing. I have every street and every open space covered with intersecting fire. There will be no place for the soldiers to hide. When they realize that, they will retreat so they can regroup. And the only way for them to retreat will be to leave the way they entered, here and here." He jabs at the ground again with the point of his knife. "You should not begin firing, Lubo, until the clear majority of the soldiers start to go down the slopes toward the valley. Then you will have them. They will be completely in the open. You will be firing down on them, and you can use everything you have, even mortars. You will cut them to pieces."

"You seem convinced that they will do exactly what you expect them to do," answers Lubo.

"Have I been wrong about them yet?"

Lubo sucks on the cigar for a moment, then mutters, "No."

"Then I won't be wrong this time either."

"Let's hope not," says Lubo, dropping the cigar and then stepping on it with the heel of his boot. "What if they bring in planes?"

"I doubt it. First of all, I'm sure they think that Megiddo is all but uninhabited. They'll take the usual precautions, but the precautions will all be on the ground, not from the air. But even if I'm wrong, planes would have a hard time making a pass at Megiddo. It's too close to the mountains. If they came in to strafe or bomb, they would not have enough time or space to pull out of their attack patterns. Even if they came from the flanks, they would still face the danger of hitting the mountains. Either way there is too much danger to order an air attack. You of all people should know that." He pauses. "And *they* know that. And they also know that the Americans would not be happy if it became known that they used American equipment on a mission like this. The Americans made it clear that the aircraft they gave could be used only for defense. Attacking a village on the border is not defense."

"What the hell do they care about defense?" Lubo shouts. "Caseres does what he wants, and the Americans finally accept it. Caseres could piss in the mouth of America, and America would call it wine."

"That may be true, but I'm just telling you the facts."

While Lubo removes another cigar from his tunic pocket and lights it, the Corsican faces Hull and Sabertes. They are both intently studying the map.

"Who will give the order to open fire after the soldiers enter the village?" asks Hull.

"That will depend on whether they try to infiltrate the village all at one time or do it a squad at a time. My instinct is that they will move through the village as a unit in one sweep," the Corsican answers. "Since you and Sabertes and I will not be in visual contact with one another, my decision to open fire will depend on when the soldiers are about to encounter the men we have posted here, here and here and here. But once the firing starts, everyone should begin firing immediately. The whole village should just erupt at once before the soldiers have a chance to realize what's happening. That way we'll hit as many as possible in the intersecting fields of fire that we've plotted. If they remain true to their practices, they will try to take their dead and wounded back with them. That will string out their retreat even longer. But we must keep firing until the very last soldier leaves the village. Then it will be up to Lubo."

"What if the soldiers decide to stay in the village, and we have to fight them house to house?" asks Sabertes.

"They won't," says the Corsican. "House-to-house fighting is not to their taste. They like to fight only when they have all the

advantages. If they stay and fight on our terms, that will give us all
the advantages. They won't choose the second option."

"You talk as if you wrote their book on tactics," interrupts
Lubo.

"I've studied their tactics for months. That's enough."

"What if they use . . . flame?" asks Hull.

"That's always a possibility. That is why you must tell your
men to target the flamethrower first. He must be targeted from
the start. And he should be easy to target. Remember, he must
expose himself in order to use his weapon. That's why you must
eliminate him from the beginning. After that, all you have to
worry about are grenades. That's why I said before that the firing must erupt all at once and be maintained. The soldiers must
not have the opportunity to react. We must put them in a state
of panic quickly." He waits and looks at each of the three men in
turn. "Any questions?" He glances suspiciously at Lubo and at the
automatic rifle he is carrying. "Why did you have to bring your
weapon with you?"

"Not my weapon," answers Lubo. "It's my power." He smiles
and taps the barrel with his open palm. "You know what the
Chinaman said—'Power comes from the barrel of a gun.'" He
laughs and pats the stock as if it were the neck of his pet dog. Then
he walks to the door and leaves without another word.

"Can we rely on him?" asks Hull.

"Absolutely. He hates Caseres more than we do. It doesn't
matter what he thinks of us. He'll do what he has to do when it's
time." The Corsican stares at both men one last time and starts to
erase the map on the floor with both hands.

"Do you know what Megiddo means?" asks Sabertes while
staring down at the disappearing map.

"Does it mean anything?" asks the Corsican.

"It's from the Bible. It's the name of the place where the last of
all battles will be fought."

"Every battle is the last battle," answers the Corsican and wonders immediately what made him say what he said. Then he remembers that Joseph had used almost the same words in their conversation a few hours earlier.

"It makes me believe that it is our destiny to be here," says Sabertes.

"Do you expect the sun to stand still while we're fighting them, Father?" asks Hull and adds, "I think it says that in the Bible too." He waits for an answer, but Sabertes has taken the remark personally and does not respond. "Forget I said that, Father," Hull adds contritely.

"You should not call me anything but Sabertes."

"I'm sorry," Hull says as he stands. "No matter what the name of this place means, this is as good a place to have it out with them as anywhere. Besides, where else is there for us to be?"

27

LUBO BASED HIS ALLIANCES on an old proverb he had learned as a child: "The enemy of my enemy is my friend." It made for short-lived alliances in most instances, but this was the way that Lubo preferred such relationships to be. It preserved the one aspect of his life and his resistance that he demanded above all others: independence.

When word was brought to him that a small group of rebels were planning an ambush for Caseres' soldiers in Megiddo and that they needed his assistance, he was initially skeptical. He husbanded his forces prudently, and he rarely committed them to a battle or a skirmish unless all the advantages were on his side. The idea of helping a small force fight a static battle did not appeal to him. If they were intent on making Megiddo itself the locale of the ambush, then they were trapped in Megiddo. They would be fighting with their backs to the wall.

Lubo believed in mobility. Attack and disappear. Attack and disappear. It was necessary when you were fighting those who outnumbered you and whose arms were superior to your own. You tried to make them fight on your terms, not theirs. You strove to make your meetings as equal as possible, if only for a brief time. Then you withdrew before they could bring their superiority to bear. It was a tactic that Lubo learned from playing chess, from watching clever boxers, from reading about American Indians and how they fought the whites in the United States.

He had heard about the Corsican and knew that he was not a fool. He knew that he would not put himself in a position that left him with no options. So, even though he differed with the Corsican on tactics, he found sufficient similarities with him on strategy to meet with him and discuss the upcoming battle and his place in it. But he finally agreed to participate in the way that the Corsican described. After all, Lubo thought at the time, what was the risk? He would be in the mountains above the village, and he knew the terrain so well that he could traverse it at midnight. He could easily escape with his men if the battle turned against the defenders in Megiddo. And if it went according to plan, he would have a chance to deal another defeat to Caseres' soldiers. That, and only that, mattered to Lubo. Both of his brothers had died in Caseres' prisons, and one of his uncles had been tortured, and his memories of those atrocities left him with a permanent disposition toward revenge. His arrangements with the Corsican simply created another opportunity for that revenge to manifest itself.

Lubo saw his life as an endless struggle with the government. It never occurred to him that he would win. In fact, something within him hoped that victory would never come since victory would bring to an end his life as a guerrilla. It was as a guerrilla commander that Lubo felt totally in his element. He knew how to lead men, to make them willing to sacrifice for a common purpose, to get results. And he could not help but be partial to a life where he retained all the initiatives. Before, during, or after a battle, his word was law, and he was simultaneously legislator and enforcer.

In his more philosophical moments, Lubo realized that victory would inevitably precipitate him into political life though he had nothing but contempt for politicians. Politics for him was an occupation for effeminate men. It seemed to him a mixture of compromise, flattery, deception, and guile. As a guerrilla fighter, he liked definite friends and definite enemies. In politics such identities became blurred so that today's enemies could emerge as tomorrow's friends and vice versa. Alliances seemed destined to be based on expediency, not conviction.

No matter what would happen in the coming battle, Lubo knew that he would continue to fight as he had always fought. The Corsican and his group would either be dead or would survive and move on to other battlefields in other countries. They could choose their enemies. But for Lubo there was only one enemy, and there was no other country. The mountains were his element. They shielded him. Whenever he planned a foray, they yielded their rugged advantages to him. And in the mountains, he knew exactly what he was doing and what he had to do. He would leave politics to others, even though he knew for certain that there would be no others.

But for the moment there were other things to think about. From his ledge in the mountain above Megiddo, he surveyed the long valley where the soldiers would come at dawn if they decided to come at all. With his automatic rifle slung from his shoulder and his pistol holstered at his hip, he felt like the king of his world.

28

CASERES AND RADAMES STAND in the center of the stadium and turn slowly full circle so that they can see all the trappings for the upcoming ceremony. National pennons flare from all the ramparts. Caseres' personal flag dominates each quadrant of the stadium. Bunting trims the barriers at the base of the stadium, and all the seats converge on a raised platform where Caseres and Radames are standing and surveying everything around them.

"Don't you think it's overdone?" asks Radames.

Caseres flicks his right hand as if the statement is not worthy of an answer. "Overdone?" he responds finally. "It's not enough." He walks from one end of the platform to the other, pacing it off as if he is measuring it. "You'll learn one day, Radames, that people love spectacle. The bigger the spectacle, the more they are impressed. The secret for us is to let spectacle work in our favor. Hitler showed the way. He would have his appearances staged with thousands of people involved. Soldiers, musicians, children. He created an event, and the event spoke for itself. He conducted it like a maestro. The people were not just an audience for him. He made them a part of what was happening. And he conducted it all. He knew the spectacle of it would make sure it would be remembered. People screamed and applauded and saluted and even wept. That's what spectacle can do for you. Remember that. That much we owe to Hitler.

He was a genius that way. Otherwise he was shit. And do you know why?"

"No."

"He died without a son. That's why."

Radames looks away, realizing that the point has been made for his benefit.

"Hitler wanted everything to begin and end with him," says Caseres and pauses. "No vision." He crosses the platform again and stands directly in front of Radames. He removes the vial of glycerin tablets from his pocket and holds it up so that Radames has to look directly at it. "Do you see this?"

"What is it?"

"Glycerin. I'm living on this. Or rather I'm kept alive by this. Do you understand that? Sometimes I take four or five of these tablets a day. Sometimes more, sometimes less. I have to keep my temper under control. I can't get excited. If I forget myself, something closes in my chest, and I can't breathe. It's as if someone is choking me." He holds up his hand and tightens it into a fist so fiercely that his knuckles bulge and whiten. "One of these days, these tablets are not going to save me." He lowers his hand and grips Radames with both hands by his shoulders.

"We have to talk, Radames. Important things will be put in motion tomorrow, and they will influence your future."

"But the festival is not until the day after tomorrow."

"I'm not talking about that." He lowers his hands. "I'm talking about Megiddo. I've ordered that Megiddo be silenced once and for all. It will be taken and destroyed completely. And that is what will happen tomorrow."

"Why? Didn't the bombardment last week destroy that village?"

"Not the way I want it to be destroyed. I don't want to leave one stone on a stone. When I know that Megiddo is nothing but a bare spot on the mountain and that there is not a soul left there, I'll be happy."

"But suppose the guerrillas just find another village and continue to be a problem for us?"

"Let them. I will do the same thing to them wherever they go." Caseres walks to the end of the platform and down the stairs. Radames follows him, and they continue up the aisle and out of the stadium. The black limousine from the embassy is parked and waiting there with Ambassador Nesbitt in the back seat. For a moment, Caseres looks surprised. As he and Radames approach the limousine, Ambassador Nesbitt asks, "Is there anything else we have to discuss?"

"No," snaps Caseres, not stopping as he continues walking toward his car. "Did you come all this way just to ask me one question?"

"I just wanted to make sure that nothing was overlooked." He tells his chauffeur to drive away. As the limousine passes Caseres, the ambassador says, "Until tomorrow then."

Once he is seated beside Radames in his own car, Caseres orders his driver to return to the capital.

"I was going back to the villa tonight," says Radames.

"You can go back after we talk. This is the one night that is ours. I want to talk to you about everything. I want to tell you everything you should know. I have to tell you all this while I can."

29

AS HE CLIMBS BACK DOWN to his bivouac in the mountain above Megiddo, Lubo wonders about each of the men he has just seen. The priest named Sabertes he remembers from his time with the cadre. In the beginning he had wondered why a priest would want to involve himself in the resistance, but he soon put away his suspicions. The man seemed not only dedicated but determined to make a contribution, and in one or two skirmishes he showed he was not a coward. But after his capture, he was never quite the same. Since he was the only one released, he gave the impression that he felt responsible for the deaths of those who were captured with him. Lubo concludes that it this sense of responsibility that explains why Sabertes is in Megiddo. Perhaps he couldn't stand the feelings of personal guilt any more. Perhaps the only way he could be at peace with himself was to place himself some- where where he would be under maximum risk. Finally Lubo just accepts the priest as one more man against Caseres. One man is like another. A soldier is a soldier.

Hull is a mystery to him. Lubo knew of the American long before he met him. He had heard stories about the hairless man who had come to Megiddo as a teacher. He was told how devoted the children were to him and how all the men and women in the village had accepted him as one of their own even though his knowledge of their dialect was meager. Still they trusted him and were proud of "their American." In the various raids that Lubo mounted from Megiddo, Hull always looked the other way as if Lubo's business were none of his business. And that remained true until all the children were killed in the bombardment. After that Hull seemed to become another man entirely. Lubo detected in Hull from then on the same spirit he detected in himself when he was provoked and when he was leading his squad of guerrillas into the interior on a mission. And somehow he knew by an inexplicable intuition that Hull at heart was a soldier and that he was and would always be an excellent soldier, intelligent and thorough and, when necessary, merciless. But why Hull has chosen to remain in a doomed village strikes Lubo as unintelligent—something an experienced soldier would not willingly do? But Hull has chosen to stay, regardless. For Lubo that doesn't make sense.

The Corsican is totally unlike Sabertes and Hull. He had gone on several missions with Lubo but always as a kind of onlooker whose advice would be sought when needed. Lubo knew that the Corsican understood explosives, and he called on him several times to inspect booby traps. Lubo studied him for both his strengths and weaknesses. He appeared to be a man without feelings. He did not drink. He showed no need for women—nor for men, for that matter. He possessed something of the tiredness of an artist facing a challenge that only he could meet, and the tiredness was there because he knew the challenge was unavoidable and not transferable. In all of their deliberations on tactics, Lubo never knew the Corsican to be wrong about anything. He knew the logic of battle in all its calibrations. He knew how much to expect from men in combat. He knew the firepower of all the weapons they would use and how to deploy them to their maximum advantage. He reminded Lubo of those Germans who had been chosen and trained by Hitler for soldiery from the time of childhood, who knew nothing else and who, after the war, dispersed all over the globe to end up as mercenaries in Argentina or as volunteers in the French Foreign Legion or as military advisors in the Middle East, peddling the only thing they really knew. But the difference between the Corsican and those who knew only soldiering was that the Corsican understood the battle tactics that could be used by revolutionaries, and he adapted and modified them accordingly.

On one occasion when there was a proclamation that Caseres would be willing to grant an amnesty to the guerrillas if they conceded that they would function only as a political party within the largely diversified and miniscule opposition that Caseres tolerated as a sop to the Americans, the Corsican told Lubo to concede nothing. He reminded Lubo that those who never conceded a thing would eventually be victorious as they had been in every revolution in recorded history. When Lubo asked him what else he had to do to be victorious, the Corsican smiled and said flatly, "Survive. Outlive your enemies."

Once back in his bivouac, Lubo cannot take his eyes off the village. Even in darkness he can see its outlines blanched by a low moon. Then he looks beyond Megiddo to the valley where the attack will come. He has a clear view of the two points of entry and an equally clear view of the slopes beyond. When Caseres' soldiers are retreating down the slopes, he will order to his men to open fire. He will use every weapon he has. It will be like target practice.

30

IT IS SEVERAL HOURS since he met with Radames at the stadium, and Caseres is sitting on his balcony. He is thinking about his wife in her apartment on the Boulevard des Grands Augustin in Paris. Another world, he thinks. A world away.

The look on her face when he told her five years before that she had no place in his plans was the same look he saw in the face of Radames when he informed him that he would be giving him more and more of his duties as premier. Radames looked at him with the same expression of total incomprehension. It was the look of a man who had just been told that he would have to swim alone after years of swimming with assistance but who had never given serious thought to doing it solo. Similarly, Caseres' wife could not understand why he was sending her away. She had tried to do everything that was expected of her, had tried to ignore the open gossip about the women that Caseres brought regularly to the palace, had let Caseres raise Radames according to his standards, had learned how to smile in public even when she had no reason to smile. Nothing seemed to satisfy him. Caseres regarded her as he might regard an overcoat that had given him good service once but that he had outgrown. Rather than throw the coat away, he decided it would be better if he just "retired" it. And so on a quiet night, he had his wife and all her belongings taken on a special plane bound for Orly and from there to an apartment he had purchased for her on the Boulevard des Grands Augustin.

After she was settled in Paris, he informed her that he had deposited the equivalent of $10 million in gold certificates in a special account in the Bank of Locarno for her use. That was his only commitment to her except for the generous amount he had given her in cash when she left. Several times during the first year she pleaded with him by mail and telephone to bring her back, but he never responded. Finally, the pleas stopped coming. For more than three years, the sum of $10 million in Locarno was never touched. Then at the beginning of the fourth year, Caseres' received notices that a specific amount was being withdrawn on a monthly basis by his wife. That assured him that she was resigned to her exile, and he paid no further attention to the matter.

31

DURING HER FIRST MONTHS IN PARIS, Caseres' wife never set foot outdoors. The domestic help that came with her apartment took care of the shopping, the housekeeping, the preparation of meals. She rarely saw them, and, when she did, she barely paid attention to them. So desolated was she by the way in which Caseres had her spirited out of the country that she could not bring herself to face people. She took her meals in her bedroom, refused all telephone calls, never even unpacked her clothes that had been trunked and transported on the plane that brought her.

At the end of the third month, she placed a telephone call to Caseres. She was told brusquely that he was unavailable. She called daily for a week and received the same message. Finally, she wrote a carefully phrased letter in which she said she could not live the rest of her life like this—away from her country, her friends, her son, him. The letter was returned to her unopened. Three other letters just like it were returned the same way.

Slowly but unrelentingly her loneliness and self-pity were replaced by chagrin. Twice she received notification from an official in the Bank of Locarno who had been ordered to make available to her whatever she needed from a special deposit of $10 million in her name. She tore the first notification into pieces so tiny that they seemed like ashes in her hands. The second notice she read and then forgot about.

Informed by her housekeeper that he could no longer receive credit for food and other necessities that were required to maintain her in the apartment, she gave him enough from the funds that Caseres had her take with her when she left. Months later she supplemented these funds by selling some of her jewelry. The revenue from this was enough to support her for more than a year.

Still she remained a recluse. The maid told her one morning that she should see the beauties of Paris or she would become as withdrawn as the famous coloratura who was also living in virtual isolation only several blocks away.

"Who is that?" she asked the maid.

"The diva from Greece. They say she is broken in her heart."

"What is her name?"

"Callas. Maria Callas."

"And she never comes out of her apartment?"

"Never," said the maid. "Sometimes when I pass her apartment in the evening, I can hear her singing. The music is very sad. She is singing by herself. For months it is like this."

A week later, the maid told Caseres' wife that Maria Callas was found dead in her apartment. Cardiac arrest. She had been dead for hours before one of the servants discovered her.

The image of Maria Callas dying in her apartment was an image that Caseres' wife could not shake. It haunted her for days. It gave her nightmares. One morning, feeling that she had to break out of the prison of herself or lose her mind, she asked the maid to accompany her to a boutique she had read about on the Rue de Rivoli. She said that she needed to buy some clothes.

From then on, she gave herself more and more reasons to be in public. She attended operas. She built up a small circle of friends who had apartments in her building. She had guests for supper. In the course of one these suppers, she discovered that she was merely one exile among many. It seemed that Paris had a way of attracting and accommodating them all. One night she was introduced to the king of Yugoslavia, a person she did not know existed. Shortly after that she met a Russian prince and his family. The prince wore an assortment of medals on his tuxedo. On another evening she was introduced to a Palestinian banker. She said as diplomatically as she could, "But there is no Palestine any longer." The banker smiled at her indulgently and said in slow, even tones, "Wherever I exist, Palestine exists."

At the end of her third year in Paris, she informed the bank official in Locarno that she wanted him to release modest sums from interest generated by the $10 million account to her directly. Careful never to cut into the principal, she learned to live prudently within her means on the collected interest, and her income for this proved to be more than ample.

She kept abreast of news from her country. Caseres was still firmly in power, but the forces of resistance in the mountains near the border seemed to be growing. At one point, citing the dangers of anarchy, Caseres dissolved the largely impotent political parties and announced that he would rule by fiat until the people became mature enough to choose their own government. When would such a choice be offered? Caseres gave no date. It was rumored that Caseres and the country's most famous singer were lovers, but none of the rumors could be confirmed.

Caseres' wife had never become involved in the politics of her country. Knowing the passions that struggles for power released, she feared what she simply did not understand. She had been merely a ceremonial presence at Caseres' side when he required her to be there, but otherwise she had no contact with the political side of her husband's life at all.

One morning she happened to be reading a copy of *Paris Match* while she was sitting under a dryer at her beautician's. On the cover was a photograph of Caseres. He was pictured on a balcony of the palace as he spoke to a crowd that looked to be numbered in the thousands. She opened the magazine until she found the five-page article that accompanied the photograph. It was basically an interview with two of Caseres' opponents, both in exile in Paris. She recognized one of the two men. He was regarded as an outstanding orator, and she remembered that Caseres had feared his ability to rouse the people against him.

"One man who can stir the people to his way of thinking," he told her once, "is worth more than an army and navy combined."

She read on, noting that the orator was never once quoted in the article while the second man was quoted at length. The second man made reference to the fact that the orator was the uncle of a resistance fighter named Lubo who was engaging Caseres' forces in a punitive guerrilla war that was ongoing. Finally, when Caseres' wife reached the final page of the article, it became clear why the orator had not been quoted. It was noted that the orator had been imprisoned by Caseres for "anti-governmental" activity. He had been kept in solitary confinement for half a year, then asked to renounce his opposition to the regime. He refused. After being tortured, he still refused. Then his torturers cut out his tongue at the root and subsequently deported him to Paris.

Caseres' wife closed the magazine and let it fall to the floor. Her hands were still quivering when the attendant returned to remove the dryer.

32

THE TWO FARMERS tell the women who are caring for the old man and boy with the broken leg in the village that they will be back. Each of them is carrying a bucket, and each of the buckets is filled to within an inch of its lip with oil. The men walk carefully so as not to spill any of the oil as they leave the village and head back to the road. When they finally reach the road, they set down the buckets and squat on the berm.

"This is not the best s-s-s-spot," says the first farmer, who speaks in a slow whisper until he begins to stammer. Whenever he stammers, he sucks in his breath and tries to repeat the word that stopped him.

"Where else should we go?" answers the other.

"I think it is b-b-b-better at the curve. No r-r-r-railing is there. If a c-c-c-car goes out of control there, it will go over the embankment and into the s-s-s-sea. There is n-n-n-nothing to stop it."

Both men rise and lift the buckets of oil and carry them carefully to the curve. Once there they set the buckets down side by side. The stammering farmer walks farther along the curve as if he is measuring something. His companion is looking at the buckets and wondering if they have brought enough oil for the job.

"I don't think we have enough oil," he tells his companion when he returns.

"We have enough if we d-d-d-don't waste any. It will not take much. But we can't w-w-w-waste a drop."

"What if we put the oil on the road, and the wrong car comes?"

"There is only one c-c-c-car that Radames drives—the white one. He will have to come back to the village this w-w-w-way."

"But it's getting dark. We won't be able to see the car in time."

"We don't need that much time." He walks back to the spot on the road that he just measured. The spot is almost twenty meters from the buckets of oil. Then he returns and says, "I want you to s-s-s-stand over where I was j—j-j—just standing. From there you can see down the road by almost two k-k-k-kilometers. I'll stay here with the oil. As s-s-s-soon as you see Radames, just signal me."

"How do you want me to signal you?"

"Just say his name loud enough for m-m-m-me to hear you."

"Then what?"

"Then get away from the r-r-r-road so he doesn't have a chance to see you."

"Should I come back here to you?"

"No. Just run down the s-s-s-slope over there. I don't want you to get in m-m-m-my way."

"What will you do?"

"I'll spill the oil across the road after you see him and give me the s-s-s-signal." He lifts both buckets of oil and places them even closer to the road. "Now you go w-w-w-where I told you to go and keep l-l-l-looking for Radames. But be sure. We don't w-w-w-want to pick the wrong car."

"How long will we have to wait?"

"Until he c-c-c-comes."

33

"ARE YOU SURE they will attack at dawn?" Joseph asks the Corsican.

The Corsican looks at him as if the question is its own answer. "As sure as I am that these mountains will be here tomorrow."

After a pause Joseph asks, "Why do you have to be here? You are not from our country. Why are you making our struggle your struggle?"

The Corsican smiles, "You're still young, Joseph. When you're older, you'll learn that there is only one struggle. Borders mean nothing at all in that struggle, and it's never a matter of flags."

Joseph frowns as if he is trying to understand. Finally, he just shrugs, accepting what the Corsican has told him. "If I were you, I don't think I would be here. Megiddo is so small that it's not even on our maps in school."

"Where else should I be? Where else would you want me to be?"

"Anywhere else. Not here."

"And if I were not here, who would tell these men how to fight against Caseres, how to use the weapons they have?"

"They would have to rely on themselves."

"That's where you are wrong, Joseph. Any time there is a battle, there will always be men who choose to fight. Each man may have a different reason, but the one thing they have in common is that they want to fight someone they think is their enemy.

But usually they don't know how to fight. They have bravery but not skill. And with modern weapons, bravery means next to nothing. What you have to have is skill, and that takes training. I have the skills. I know every calibration of every weapon the men have here. And besides that, I hate the bastards who will attack us tomorrow. I hate every one of them from here to the four corners of the world. Don't ask me why. I just can't stop fighting them as long as I know that one of them is still living."

"But you can't fight all of them."

"No, I can't, but I know that when I fight them here, it's the same as fighting them everywhere, and that satisfies me."

Joseph shrugs again and looks at his watch by lantern light. "There will be sun in two hours."

"Use the radio. Tell the priest and the American what you just told me. From now on nobody sleeps."

34

IT IS EXACTLY ONE HOUR before dawn when Kronos issues orders for two of the three companies of the battalion to begin their advance toward Megiddo. He estimates that it will take each of them approximately one hour to cross the valley and ascend the slopes to the village. His calculation has them arriving at the village just as the sun rises. This will put the sun at their backs, and it will leave whatever defenders there might be in Megiddo looking directly into it.

Kronos sees no reason for any unorthodox maneuvering of his troops. He has chosen a simple, classical approach. One company will advance in a loose formation of skirmishers from the right and enter Megiddo through one of its two points of entry. The other will perform the same maneuver on the left and enter Megiddo by the second gate. He and the third company will remain in reserve at the base of the slope below the village and wait for developments.

Even in the hazy darkness, Kronos can see the soldiers moving ahead on his left and right. Once they are in the valley, he can see nothing, but he can still hear them. The sound of infantry advancing is for Kronos like no other sound. Occasionally, a sound of metal against metal. Bootheels on pebbles or loose stones. A cough or two. A curse. An order. The heavy presence of men trudging heavily over terrain they are discovering as they go.

When both companies have crossed the valley and are at the base of the slope, the commanders inform Kronos by radio of their positions. Immediately Kronos orders the third company to advance, and he joins them. The valley that looked so smooth from a distance the evening before now turns treacherous. Kronos turns his ankle in a rut. He hears several soldiers trip and fall heavily.

When he finally reaches the base of the slope, he is sweating through his dungarees, and his right ankle feels as if someone has hit the bone there with a hammer.

The two company commanders of the first two companies join him in the semidarkness, and he goes over the plan of attack with them for one last time. There is to be no firing until they enter the village, and then only if they see there will be resistance. The soldiers will slip into the village through the two gates quickly so as to establish themselves inside the walls as soon as possible. Then they will clear everything, street by street, house by house, room by room. Later, the demolition men will place the charges. Kronos asks the commanders if there are any questions. The commanders shake their heads no.

From his position, Kronos watches the first and second company begin their ascent to Megiddo. The men run in a crouch and then stop before they make the next dash. They repeat this procedure again and again. Soon more than one hundred men have advanced halfway up the slope. Then one company veers toward the right gate into the village, and the other to the left.

When the first company reaches the gate, the sun is almost fully risen. The timing is exactly as Kronos estimated. Anyone waiting in the village will have to contend with a fierce, horizontal glare, and that in itself will prevent their even seeing the soldiers until most of them are in the village. Even as this thought crosses his mind, he sees the first pair of soldiers slip through the gate. Then a second pair. Then a third.

For a moment he thinks of Thermopylae again. He forces the thought from his mind, lifts his binoculars from their holster and focuses on the right gate and then the left. More than half of both companies are now inside Megiddo. He holds the binoculars in his right hand and reaches down with his left to massage his pulsing ankle.

35

USING A PERISCOPE so that none of the attackers can spot him, the Corsican focuses on the infantry approaching Megiddo. He is speaking to Hull and Sabertes by wireless as he watches.

"They are coming in two companies, one toward the south gate and the other to the west gate. No deviation in plan at all. They're doing exactly as I expected."

He rotates the periscope and squints through it again.

"There is only one company in reserve. I think it's safe to say that it will stay in reserve and let the other two enter the village. Remember. No firing. Nothing. Keep all your men out of sight. They will have time enough to get into position and open fire. But nothing premature. Nothing."

The Corsican is telling himself that it is the ambush at Kabylia all over again. Instead of defending a village then, he and his men were waiting in a gorge for the legionnaires. He had posted his men in their positions until collectively they created a kind of horseshoe. All his men had to do was wait for the legionnaires to enter the horseshoe from its open end, keep waiting until as many as possible were within the gorge, then wait a little longer until even the rear guard was enclosed in the trap. Then the Corsican gave the order to fire. In that single skirmish the legionnaires lost their entire number. The Algerians slit the throats of the six wounded prisoners. The Corsican himself escaped with only two wounded in his group, and these two had only flesh wounds that healed within days.

Later when he joined the Palestinians at Karameh, he had them follow the same tactics. They let the infantry enter the town, and then they fought them house to house, nullifying the superior fire power of the Israelis and forcing them to fight in close quarters where the odds were equal. The Israeli casualties were never truthfully reported in the Israeli press, but the Corsican knew from his own observations that more half of the invading forces had been killed.

Now as he swings the periscope to the south gate, he sees the first soldier enter and flatten himself against the village wall. He is immediately followed by a second soldier, then a third, a fourth and on and on.

" . . . four, five, eight, fifteen. They are coming in steadily now." He pauses and shifts the periscope a fraction. "So far they are not coming directly toward us. They are fanning out along the wall. Yes. Yes. Now I see what they are doing. They are going to come through the streets in a cordon. In a cordon. Do you hear me? And that's all to the good. They'll need to get as many men as possible through the gate before they try that. Fifty. Sixty, maybe . . . "

When he turns the periscope to the west gate, he sees the same pattern developing. He smiles to himself and turns to Joseph.

"They are doing exactly what they were trained to do, Joseph. All of them must have studied from the same field manuals."

"How long before we shoot them?"

"You leave the shooting to the others, Joseph."

"How long before they shoot them?"

"Not long. Two or three minutes. Maybe less. It's up to the enemy. It depends on when the soldiers decide to start through the village."

36

WHILE SABERTES IS LISTENING to the Corsican on his wireless, he can see exactly what the Corsican is describing. He has a
clear view of the south gate, and he watches soldier after soldier
enter in a running crouch and take a defensive position against the
wall. Knowing that his position will be the first point of contact
with the attackers since he is closer to the wall than Hull or the
Corsican, he surveys the men he has positioned to his left and
right. Like him they are watching the soldiers at the gate, but at
quick intervals they look at Sabertes, waiting for him to give them
the signal to commence firing. Sabertes in turn concentrates again
on the south gate and listens to the Corsican's voice on the radio.

" . . . more of them at the south gate than the west gate. They
will probably begin advancing on your side first, Sabertes." There
is a pause. "Hull, can you hear what I'm saying? The soldiers will
probably make contact with Sabertes first. But once there is the
first contact, the first shot, the first anything, we will all begin
firing. Make every shot count. Aim at their heads."

Sabertes checks to make sure that the safety catch is released
on his weapon. When he looks again at the south gate, he sees
the soldiers starting to approach his position. They are actually
erect as they come closer, taking no advantage at all of anything that could be used as cover. He assumes that they think
no one is in the village at all. Then he notices how each of the
soldiers is carrying his rifle at the ready and that bayonets are

attached to the barrels. A flamethrower is in the exact center of the approaching line.

"You're lucky, Sabertes," the Corsican is saying on the radio. "They think no one is here. They're coming toward you at a walk. It should be easy for you . . . "

The first shot comes as such a surprise to Sabertes that he drops his weapon. Then he realizes that the advancing soldiers must have made contact with his forward observers. At that moment, he sees the soldiers come to a complete stop. A few crouch, but the rest simply stand their ground as if the shot they heard might have been a mistake. They are still standing when the fusillade from the men to the right and left of Sabertes targets them. Sabertes watches them topple or lurch sideways or simply drop when the bullets hit them. It is like an execution. Inexplicably the flamethrower is not hit, and he fires burst after burst of orange fire before Sabertes himself shoots him in the leg and then just below the throat. But the flames have already spattered the men on his left flank, and Sabertes hears the screams of men whose flesh is burning. Now he can hear rifle fire and automatic fire from the center of the village and from the east, and he knows that the Corsican and Hull have now joined the battle. The screams of the burning men do not stop.

37

HULL ORDERS HIS MEN to begin firing just a few seconds after he hears the first shot from the south gate. The first three soldiers in the advancing party drop instantly. The ones behind them look left and right for some place to hide or hide behind. Like those who advanced on Sabertes, these soldiers began their sweep in full view of Hull and his men on the assumption that the village was completely deserted. One of the advantages they have in Hull's section of the perimeter is that there are more buildings still standing, and, once they realize the trap they are in, they immediately sprint into the buildings and start to return fire.

After ten minutes of intense crossfire, Hull realizes that the skirmish will become a standoff. He calls his second in command and tells him that the men should use grenades.

The first grenade hits the wall of one of the houses and rolls back into the middle of an alleyway before it bursts. Other grenade explosions soon follow, and for a few moments the sound of the explosions overpowers everything else.

Hull knows that this is the time for his men to attack in order to exploit not only the surprise of the first volleys but the shock of the explosions on the attackers. He signals to his second in command to lead his men from the right while he takes the rest of the men with him to the left.

"Don't shoot until you're sure you have a target," says Hull. "We don't want to end up shooting at one another."

What Hull will remember of the next ten minutes will not be the way he led five men around the rubble on his left flank and how they totally surprised more than a dozen soldiers who were still firing at the position where Hull and the men had been. Nor will he remember how his men fired at the soldiers with an intensity that revenge alone could explain. All he will remember will be the soldier who somehow survived the rifle fire but who was writhing and bleeding from wounds in both legs when Hull discovered him. Then he will remember how he, thinking suddenly of the broken bodies of the children he had removed from the bombarded school and how he and the other villagers buried them side by side in one huge hole, stood above the bleeding soldier, removed his pistol from his holster and fired six bullets into the soldier's face and chest with a calmness that astonished him.

38

"WHY AREN'T WE SHOOTING at them?" asks Joseph.

"Not yet, Joseph," answers the Corsican. "Not quite yet."

Even as he speaks, the Corsican is listening to the firefight on his right flank between Hull and the soldiers who entered by the west gate as well as a similar firefight between Sabertes and soldiers who came through the south gate. He can see through the aperture of his periscope that some of the soldiers who have been caught in the crossfire are collapsing toward the center of the village, and it is here that the Corsican has concentrated the firepower of the men under his command. He decides that he will wait until as many soldiers as possible are in enfilade before he gives the signal to commence firing. He smiles to himself as he sees that his tactics are working out exactly as he planned. Actually the plan is one that he learned years earlier while studying intertribal warfare in Africa. One of the tribes had perfected the maneuver of luring the enemy between two flanking positions. The warriors on either flank would remain quiet and hidden until the enemy was well within the trap or, as they put it, "within the horns." Then they would attack, forcing the enemy to move deeper "into the loins" where other fighters were waiting for them. The crucial component was to cut off all possibility of retreat or escape so as to give the maneuver maximum effectiveness. For his purposes, the Corsican had decided early in his preparation that the two narrow gates into Megiddo were not designed to accommodate the flight of desperate soldiers retreating in panic.

"Joseph, I want you to contact Lubo."

"Now?"

"Now."

"What will I say to him?"

"After you reach him, I will talk to him."

The Corsican sees that more than forty soldiers have gravitated toward the center of the village. He checks to see that his own men, who are crouched behind the rubble between the central fountain and the church, are still holding their fire. He squints through the periscope just in time to notice that the reserve company is starting to advance up the slope to the south and west gates. Slowly he raises his automatic rifle to the edge of the parapet and trains his sights on the first soldier he sees. His shot will be the prearranged signal for the rest of the men to fire at will. Without even caring if his shot will strike the soldier in his sights or not, he fires. The soldier lurches to his right and sprawls. A second after the Corsican fires, all of his men commence firing.

Realizing that they are completely exposed, the soldiers begin to disperse in different directions. Some at the perimeter drop their weapons and dash for the south gate while others rush to the west gate. A few make it, but most of the others are hit on the way. Regardless, more and more of the soldiers, knowing that they are doomed if they stay, sprint for the gates.

"Do you have Lubo, Joseph?"

"He is waiting to talk to you, sir."

The Corsican takes the speaker from Joseph and, as if he making a social call, says calmly, "Lubo?"

"I can see everything from here," Lubo answers. "Your plan is working perfectly. Congratulations."

"The soldiers who made it through the gates are heading back down the slope. Can you see them?"

"I can see them. But there are soldiers coming up the slope as well."

"That is the reserve company. They were there for support."

"Is that a bonus for us?"

"A total bonus. You can use your mortars and strafe them at the same time. There is no place for them to hide."

39

WHEN THE FIRST MORTAR ROUNDS explode on the slope, Kronos realizes that his advance platoons are completely exposed. All they can do is crouch and sprawl on the spines of the slope while the barrages of round after round from the mortars hit and create deadly volcanic upheavals around them. Some of them run toward the south and west gates of Megiddo in a kind of blind obedience to the mission they were trained to complete while others start a disorganized retreat back down the slope to the base position where Kronos himself is watching them. None of them makes it down. The mortar rounds and the strafing fire are so frequent and concentrated that all of them are cut down in midrun.

Kronos leaves his position and hurries to the side of the first wounded soldier he can find. He tries to drag him back down the slope. By the time he reaches his position, he just has enough time to pull the man behind a rock when a mortar round detonates above the two of them. Kronos feels himself being lifted and hurled to his right. When he hits the ground, he is panting. He touches his legs, his chest, his legs, and his face to make sure he is still intact. Then he looks at the wounded soldier he tried to save and sees that the protecting rock, having been dislodged by the blast, has toppled on him. All he can see of the soldier are his arms and legs extending from beneath the rock as if it crushed him in the manner of some primitive form of execution.

Kronos hears the incessant fire of automatic weapons. He turns over on his elbows and surveys the slope above him. From high above Megiddo, someone is strafing the slope with a machine gun. Kronos watches helplessly as the bullets hit the dead as well as the few who are wounded. The bodies of the dead soldiers lurch when they are killed a second time and then settle in a new and even more awkward repose. Kronos continues to watch until the firing becomes more sporadic and then stops completely. In the lull he waits and watches for any of the soldiers to move. He studies each of the bodies in turn to see if a head turns or a finger stirs, but there is no movement whatsoever.

Edging into a small ditch until he is sure that he is out of sight of anyone who might be watching from Megiddo or from the mountain above it, Kronos removes his wireless from his belt.

"Major Kronos here! Major Kronos here! Can you read me? Can you read me? Over."

He pauses and waits. He can hear static on the receiver. It mounts to a steady growl. Meanwhile Kronos listens to the resumption of automatic fire not only on the slope but from Megiddo as well.

"Major Kronos here! Can you read me? Over," he shouts into the wireless.

The growl lessens. The airwaves become so static-free for a moment that Kronos shakes the wireless to make sure it is still working.

The voice on the receiver startles him with its clarity.

"Come in, Major Kronos. This is battalion headquarters."

"Megiddo," Kronos mutters. "Megiddo was an ambush. We are . . ."

"Have you taken casualties?"

"It's a disaster."

"Have you completed the mission?"

"Didn't you hear me? The mission is a disaster. Both of my advance platoons are probably still in the village if they aren't already dead. I have no way of knowing what happened to them. The reserve platoon is trapped on the slope below the damn village. It's hard for me to know from where I am if there are any survivors. The fire is relentless, and it is continuing. As far as I know, I'm the only one left."

"What about those in the village?"

"Didn't you hear what I said? I have no way of knowing what happened to them."

"How many of the enemy are still in Megiddo?"

"What the hell are you talking about? How can I know that unless my own men tell me, and they're probably all dead. Can't you understand that? I'm not in touch with my platoon commanders or my company commanders. Is that clear?" He waits for a response. "I may have some wounded here. I don't know."

"What shall we tell Premier Caseres? He insisted on being kept abreast of the attack."

"Tell him we were completely surprised. Tell him the important thing now is that we have to deal with the wounded and the dead. We can't just leave them." He is breathing heavily. "It was a total disaster. There's no other way to put it."

"That's not what the premier was expecting. I can tell you that."

"That's not what I was expecting either, God damn it. I've lost my whole command."

"Where are you now, Major?"

"I'm approximately forty or fifty yards from the base of the slope in a small gulley."

"Stay there. I'll be back to you after I've reported this news to the premier. Over."

40

"WHAT ARE YOU TELLING ME?" shouts Caseres into the mouth-piece of his telephone. "Listen! This is unacceptable! Don't interrupt me! This is absolutely unacceptable! I want that village turned into ashes! Ashes! I don't care what is required!"

Caseres slams the phone into its cradle and turns to Radames.

"Can you believe this?" he shouts, not so much at Radames but at the world at large. "Hundreds of my best soldiers cannot take a village! A village!"

"What are you going to do?" asks Radames tentatively.

Caseres clasps his hands behind his back and begins to pace the room in a slow circle. When he has completed the third circle, he stops and glares at his son.

"In tactics, Radames, you begin with right now and go backward from what is not acceptable. In this case a defeat is not acceptable. Therefore, we do whatever is necessary to avoid defeat." He lifts the phone from its cradle. "Connect me with General Ord at the airbase. Quickly."

"Are you going to use planes?" asks Radames.

"Yes."

"What about the Americans? You heard what the American ambassador said would happen if you use their equipment."

"If I listened to the Americans . . . " Caseres begins. Then he cocks the phone to his ear. "Ord? I want you to listen to me very carefully. The ground attack on Megiddo has been repulsed.

Yes. I know. I can't understand it either, but I have just received a report that we've taken major losses there. We've failed. The village is still in the hands of the rebels." He pauses and looks at Radames, then resumes his conversation with Ord. "I want you to arm six aircraft with the new missiles we've gotten from the Americans. Yes. The ones from the Americans. I want that done immediately." He pauses. "As soon as they are armed, I want you to order a mission against Megiddo. Use your best pilots. And when . . . " He holds the telephone at arm's length for a moment then brings it back. "What do you mean you can't mount an attack against Megiddo?" He pauses again, listening. "I don't give a damn about the mountains. Are you telling me that your pilots are not good enough to launch their missiles and avoid the mountains? Is that what you're saying?" He listens. "Enough of that, Ord. I want those planes in the air within the hour. One hour!" He waits. "Let me worry about the Americans. I don't care if they see the planes being readied. Are we taking orders in our own country from the Americans? Whose flag are you serving, Ord?" He waits again. Then he nods as he listens. "That's exactly correct. I will not accept failure, do you hear? I will not accept failure. If those pilots come back without having the done the job, I want the planes refueled and rearmed and sent back. And if they fail again, I want it done a third time. You will send them back and back again until they do what must be done. I want that village removed from the face of the earth."

He hangs up the phone and turns to Radames.

"That is the way you have to deal with the military. Let that be a lesson to you. No one gives the final orders but the premier. No one."

41

"JOSEPH, WHERE IS THE PRIEST?" asks the Corsican.

Joseph points through the bunker window, and the Corsican follows the direction he has indicated until he sees Sabertes. He is just making the sign of the cross over several wounded or possibly dead soldiers at the south gate.

Shrugging, the Corsican turns to Hull and with a serious smile says, "A priest is always a priest. They never change, and you can't train it out of them." He turns again to focus on Sabertes. "And it doesn't matter if he's blessing his own men or the enemy, does it? Twenty minutes ago he was probably trying to kill the very men he's trying to save now."

"I think Sabertes had some casualties in his unit because of the flamethrower," says Hull.

"What about you?" asks the Corsican. "Did you have losses?"

"Two dead. Three wounded."

The Corsican turns to Joseph and asks, "How many did we lose, Joseph?"

"Three, sir."

"Dead?"

"Dead."

"Well, that's a good percentage," says the Corsican. "Think of the ones that Caseres lost. There must be one hundred dead and dying out there. Lubo says he strafed and mortared everyone on the slope. He used every mortar round he had." He faces Hull.

"Lubo's been scanning the slope with binoculars for almost half an hour now, and he told Joseph that nothing is moving there."

"What are you going to do with their wounded that are out there?" asks Hull.

"*Coup de grace,*" mutters the Corsican. "But not now. Not yet. Some of them may be just playing dead. They could be just waiting for us to show ourselves. As for the rest, we'll give them a little time to die. I don't want to waste ammunition."

"You mean you think that some of them will still fight?"

"Who knows? Why take the chance? They can't even see us from where they are on the slope."

"We'll have to show ourselves sooner or later."

"Later will be soon enough," says the Corsican and nods at Joseph. "You were a good boy, Joseph. You did exactly what I wanted you to do. You were a great help to me."

"I wanted to fight them, sir."

"You'll have a lot of time to fight, Joseph."

"Do you think that more soldiers will come now?"

"Not now. Once they total their losses, they won't be in a rush to come back. They might try something else next time. Not infantry."

"But how will they know what happened here?"

"Radio. Wireless. Someone must have released something to the main base."

"But what if nothing was sent?"

"Do you remember that plane that passed over the village yesterday?"

"Yes."

"He'll be back. He'll take pictures. That will tell everything. But I'm sure they have an idea already of how bad it was for them. Someone must have sent a message or even more than one. Either way they'll learn everything."

"You're damn sure they won't come back, aren't you?" asks Hull.

"I know them like a book, my friend."

"I'd hate to think you're wrong. We're ripe for a counterattack right now."

"Look through this if you don't believe me," says the Corsican and offers Hull his place behind the periscope.

Hull adjusts his right eye to the aperture and surveys the bodies on the slope and then the valley beyond. It is just at that moment that Kronos runs and dives into a small gulch that conceals him from view. Hull continues to look beyond Kronos to the valley and finally to the mountains beyond. Nothing.

"Did you see anything?" asks the Corsican.

"There's a man alive out there. I saw him running."

"I mean did you see anything that looks like a preparation for a counterattack?

"No."

"You're still in Vietnam, Hull. The people here are not like the Vietnamese. These people count their losses very carefully. They have cultivated the habit of not having to fight again if they choose not to, and they will choose not to now. With the Vietnamese, it was different. You were fighting them in their country. It was victory or subservience to them, and Uncle Ho made sure they did not forget what subservience meant in their history. They would have fought you to the last man."

The Corsican's logic makes Hull look away. Through the window he can still see Sabertes ministering to the same two soldiers, and he finds himself shaking his head in disbelief at the very sight of what the man is doing. But the mood passes. His experience in Vietnam has made nothing that can happen in a battle inconceivable to him.

"Joseph," says the Corsican, "tell the priest to come here."

"Why don't you just let the priest alone?" says Hull. "What harm is he doing?"

Ignoring Hull, the Corsican repeats, "Joseph, tell the priest to come here."

Without another word Joseph leaves the bunker and walks rather stealthily toward Sabertes. When he reaches him, he touches him softly on the shoulder. Sabertes looks up at him but continues to pray over one soldier who is bleeding from a wound in his neck. The soldier is gasping. The blood from the wound comes in spurts.

Hull is concentrating on Joseph and Sabertes when he hears the first plane. It bursts over the bunker and veers off. A second after it passes there is a rapid concussion of rockets detonating somewhere to the left of the south gate.

"Joseph!" shouts the Corsican. "Come back! Come back here!"

The boy turns and looks at the Corsican as the second plane comes over. Then a third. Then a fourth. A fifth. They come as fast as artillery shells. It all seems instantaneous. One minute there is nothing. Then there is the incoming scream of the jets as they make their passes and leave their echoing jet wash and boom as they pull up.

"Joseph!" shouts the Corsican. He rushes from the bunker toward Joseph, who is still standing as if dazed beside Sabertes.

Hull follows. He can see the jets vectoring in the east for another pass. He stops as if to prepare himself for what he knows is coming. The Corsican has already reached Joseph and is pulling him back to the bunker. Sabertes does not move. Hull sees the first jet peel off. He listens to the approaching whine of its dive. When the rocket hits, he sees Joseph and the Corsican separated by the blast and catapulted in opposite directions. Seconds later when Hull looks again, there is nothing where Joseph, the Corsican, Sabertes, and the wounded soldiers were but a chasm. Debris is still falling around him, and Hull can hear rocks and sprays of dirt drumming on the roof of the bunker as he crawls inside again. All the other jets are making their runs now, and the whole village is nothing but a series of explosions.

42

KRONOS WATCHES PLANE AFTER PLANE release its rockets into the village until the entire plateau of Megiddo becomes one convulsion after another. For a moment he is dazzled by the sheer accuracy of it all. Something in him admires this kind of focus and precision. Then he realizes that none of the wounded of his entire battalion has been spared in this onslaught.

He stands and starts to walk up the slope toward Megiddo when the planes return for their second sortie. This time they concentrate only on the slope, and Kronos himself is thrown backward after the first salvo. When he regains his feet, he sees that the bodies of his men have been blown to smithereens.

"Stop!" he shouts as the last plane passes.

He walks uncertainly and follows the planes as they circle in the east for what appears to be a third strike. Running to a small rise, Kronos removes his shirt and starts waving it like a flag at the planes.

"Stop! That's enough!" he shouts and waves the shirt. "You're killing my men! You're killing my men!"

He keeps on shouting as the first plane streaks toward him, releasing a bracket of rockets at the upper levels of the slope. Spumes of debris rise and fall. Each of the planes repeats the pattern. Kronos can see bodies blown into the air. He can also see that the silhouette of the village no longer caps the plateau. Even the walled gates are nothing but rubble.

"You bastards! You bastards!" he shouts at the planes. He slams the shirt into the ground as the last plane dives toward him. As it passes, the pilot discharges his rockets into the upper slope and at what is left of the village. He has ended his dive at a lower altitude than the others, and he tries to pull his plane up and away. Kronos can see what is about to happen. When the plane hits the mountain, there is a bursting cloud of flame and then nothing but a black smudge. Kronos stares at the smudge. Behind and above him, the other planes have grouped and are already heading back to their base near the capital. There is an empty space in the formation.

43

THE PILOT OF THE SPOTTER PLANE resents having been ordered to make another surveillance. The order came from the
premier himself just after the jets returned from their mission
to Megiddo. The premier wanted the destruction of the village
photographed to prove to one and all that the rebels there had
been totally routed or killed.

The pilot calculates that it has not even been twenty-four
hours since his last reconnaissance. The only difference this time
is that he is flying with a new photographer. He follows the same
flight pattern, coming in low between the mountains and staying
close to the valley floor before pulling up. Halfway across the valley, he feels the photographer nudge and point ahead to what used
to be Megiddo. The pilot cannot make out the outline of a single
building left standing, and the village wall is gapped in so many
places that it is no longer a wall at all.

When he reaches the base of the slope below the village, the
pilot puts the plane into a banking climb so that he and the photographer can see as much of Megiddo as possible. He tells the
photographer to wait until he makes a second pass before he takes
his pictures. With his left wing tipped slightly, he sustains the
climb and looks down. He sees numerous bodies both in the village and on the slope. He sees as well many craters the size of the
foundations of houses. Every structure in the village is rubble or
near rubble. Imagining the force of the onslaught from the air

that resulted in such devastation, the pilot shakes his head from side to side and sighs. Just then he puts the plane in a sharp turn to avoid the mountains. At the completion of his turn, he notices a huge black smudge on the mountainside behind the village. Then he remembers that one of the pilots had told him that another pilot in the squadron had crashed because he had not been able to pull up from his dive in time.

Readying the plane for a second pass, the pilot tells his photographer to shoot as many frames as he can. He does not want to make another run. The photographer nods and swings his camera into position.

As the pilot banks for the start of his run, he looks down in time to see a man without a shirt tramping over the debris of the ramparts toward Megiddo. He can tell from the man's trousers that he is a soldier. He points down so that the photographer will see the man as well, but the photographer is already looking at another man just emerging from what's left of a bunker near the village center. The man is completely bald, and he walks as if in a trance toward what's left of one of the gates.

"There are two men down there," says the photographer. "Do you see them?"

The pilot nods his head yes as the plane passes over the center of the village where the shirtless soldier and the bald man are now standing motionless before one another. But this is all he has time to see because at that moment a rack of gunfire from the mountains above Megiddo rips through the plane. The pilot banks the plane as sharply as he can without stalling, but the bullets are still tearing through the fabric of the fuselage. Then he hears the camera drop from the photographer's hands and bounce against the back of his seat. The photographer makes no sound, but the pilot feels the sudden slump of his body against the back of his seat as well.

The pilot tries to accelerate by leaning forward as if a small act of will is all that is needed. Seconds later he finds himself zooming across the valley, and there are no more shots. He tests the controls to make sure that the plane is still operable. Then he looks back over his seat. The photographer has fallen back, and the pilot can see the holes in his flight jacket that the bullets made when they hit him.

44

"STOP ACTING SO RESTLESS," says Caseres. He is watching Radames pick at the quick of his fingers. "Why are you that way? Do you have one of your playthings waiting for you at the villa?"

"It's not anything like that. Besides, I'm not going back to the villa until later." He paused. "I've just been working too hard lately. I'm tired."

"Work? You don't know what the word means, Radames." Caseres waits for an answer and then sips audibly from a cup of coffee. "You have too much of your mother in you. You're too used to being taken care of. And for that I'm to blame. I let you get away with too much. You never had enough responsibilities. But that's all over now. As of tonight that's all over. When we enter the stadium, I want everyone to see you with new eyes." He centers the cup on its saucer so heavily that the coffee bounces up and over the table.

"What do you want me to do?" asks Radames.

"I want you to stand beside me like a soldier. I want you to look like a premier." Caseres rises from his chair and strides to the window. Through the window the entire city is visible to the horizon. He turns to Radames and says, "Come here. Stand beside me. I want to show you something. I want to tell you something."

Radames walks hesitantly to his father and stands next to him. Caseres puts his arms around his son and points down to the city with his free hand. "Do you know what that was when I first came here? It was like a village. I came from a village in the interior, and this capital was just like the village I left, only larger. That was the only difference. It was just a larger village. That's what I found when I came here. And I vowed on my mother's grave that I would do something about it. I joined the army. I did what I had to do. I advanced. I made the right friends. I learned who my enemies were. And when I was strong enough to move against them, I moved against them with force. And at the same time, I made sure that no one could move against me. I created the best secret police network in this part of the world. That's been the work of the past thirty years. Do you understand that?"

Radames nods his head meekly in agreement.

"I turned this large village into a real capital," Caseres continues. "I convinced the Americans to finance me. I told them that I was moving the country toward democracy. That's something they always like to hear, so I said it to them over and over again. I'm still saying it, and they still believe me, and they continue to finance me. Do you understand? I want that to go on. I want that to go on when you are in my position. I want you to have everything I've earned. I don't want it go to someone else. I want the names of Caseres and Radames to be one and the same. I want those names to last forever in this country." He hugs his son against him in a one-arm embrace, but Radames does not respond. Caseres drops his arm, and the two of them return to their chairs.

"Do you want me to stay here with you now? Is there more you want to tell me?"

"I'm waiting for a telephone call. When I get it, you can leave. Then you can go wherever you want. To the villa. To your whores. Wherever. But tomorrow I want you here early in full uniform."

"You already told me that about the uniform."

"Don't forget it."

"What telephone call are you waiting for?"

"From Ord, the commander of all the squadrons near the coast." He waits. "It's about that village near the border. Megiddo. Do you remember what I told you about that?"

"Yes."

"Well, then you know what it means. The guerrillas have been using it for years to make things difficult for me, to try to destabilize the country, to try to embarrass me. So I made a decision. I decided that I never wanted to hear about Megiddo again. It had become more than a nuisance. It had turned into a symbol for those who are against us. That's why I ordered that it should be destroyed. Destroyed completely. Crushed to powder. I'm waiting for the squadron commander to call and tell me that my orders have been carried out."

"But you could have done that before? Why did you wait until today?"

"Because I wanted to be sure that there would be no distractions. I want all eyes to be on the stadium. I want everybody— especially the Americans—to know that I am the premier for life and that you will come after me. I want that seen and understood. Without distractions."

Radames nods. Again he starts to fret with the quicks of his fingers. Just then the telephone rings. Caseres hurries to the desk, lifts the receiver and puts it to his ear. He speaks quietly for a moment, then listens for a protracted period. He keeps nodding his head as he listens. Finally, he say, "Good." He replaces the receiver. Turning to Radames, he says, "That was the news I was waiting for, Radames. There will be no distractions at the stadium." He walks toward Radames. "You can go now. But be at your best at the stadium. It will be the beginning of your world."

45

"RADAMES IS NOT C-C-C-COMING," says the farmer. "We brought these buckets of oil for n-n-n-nothing. I thought he would come b-b-b-back this way."

"We've waited for him for more than twelve hours. Why should we wait any more?"

"I don't know. Maybe he w-w-w-went some other way."

"You said there is no other way."

"Or maybe he did not go b-b-b-back to the villa," says the farmer, letting his hand rest on the rim of one of the oil-filled buckets. "I don't know w-w-w-what we should do."

"Well, we've waited this long. We can wait one more hour."

"What did your w-w-w-wife tell you about the boy when she came?"

"His leg is very bad. He is crazy with the pain."

"Did anyone call a d-d-d-doctor?"

"You know that a doctor will not come here."

"Then we should t-t-t-take him to the infirmary."

"The boy is afraid they will cut his leg off if we take him."

The farmer with the stammer shakes his head from side to side, not so much in disagreement or disbelief as in futility. He looks down the long coastal road. Beyond it the sea is darkening to a deeper blue, and a star or two has already appeared at the horizon. But he sees no cars either coming from or heading to the capital.

"Should I go back to the shoulder and keep a lookout just in case?" asks the second man.

"Yes," answers the farmer. "We'll wait until m-m-m-midnight. If he hasn't come by then, we'll l-l-l-leave." He watches his companion shuffle to his position on the shoulder and squat there. The farmer pulls a cigarette from a squashed pack in his shirt pocket, lights it, and draws in the smoke as if he is smoking the last cigarette in his life. There are more stars above the horizon now, and he feels a definite calm as he watches the night take over the sea and the land. He keeps on smoking, and suddenly the stars are everywhere.

"Radames!" shouts his companion. "Radames! He is coming! He is coming!"

"Are you s-s-s-sure?"

"It's the white car! His car!"

The farmer with the stammer throws his cigarette behind him, lifts a bucket of oil in either hand and runs to the curve in the road. He sets one bucket down on the berm and, holding the other with both hands, swings it as if he might be pitching soapy water on a floor so that the oil spreads in a widening swath when it splatters. Then he lifts the second bucket and does the same. Satisfied, he runs back to the spot where he was smoking the cigarette. His companion is waiting for him there.

"I thought I told you to w-w-w-wait for me down the hill."

"What's the difference?"

"Are you sure it's R-R-R-Radames?"

"It's his car. I'm sure of it."

"Is he c-c-c-coming fast?"

"He always travels fast."

The man with the stammer listens for the sound of the oncoming motor. An instant later he sees the piercing beams of the headlights make a dawn of the dark curve in the road. Suddenly the car is passing him in a white blur, and he is just able to glimpse Radames at the wheel. The farmer stands and runs toward the road.

"Now," he shouts. "Now, now, now!"

The red taillights of the car are converging as the car speeds farther away from him and approaches the curve. With both hands clenched at his sides, the farmer sees the car moving not to the right as the curve demands but straight ahead. He sees the red lights suddenly vanish. Then there is a shattering crash of metal and glass on rock. This is followed by successive crashes. The farmer reaches the curve just in time to see the car hit the last crag above the sea. It bucks over the crag and hits the sea with a hiss. It bobs there for a moment and then simply disappears in the water.

The farmer hears his companion running to join him.

"Did we get him?" asks the man, looking down the cliff to the sea.

"Yes."

"Are you sure?"

"Yes."

The farmer walks closer to the edge of the curve. The spot is still frothing slightly where the sinking car left its own small whirlpool on the surface.

46

EN ROUTE TO MAGDALENA'S APARTMENT, Caseres tells the chauffeur, "Stop at the stadium."

The chauffeur nods and in minutes drives the Mercedes to the main gate of the stadium. The pennons all around the top rim are blowing in one direction in the night wind. The chauffeur proceeds through the main gate and maneuvers to the runner's track and makes a slow, complete lap. Caseres notes that the bunting is in place around the central pavilion, and that the seats are rayed out from it in five separate directions like the legs of a starfish. He taps the chauffeur on the shoulder.

"Stop here for a moment."

Caseres opens the car door and steps on the track. Then he walks erectly up one of the aisles to the pavilion, climbs the stairs, and stands in the exact center of the platform. He turns slowly from the north to face east, south, then west and back to north. He can still smell the aroma of the fresh lumber that he is standing on, and he rocks back and forth on his soles as if testing the platform's resilience. Then he takes a deep breath, stamps one final step on the platform and returns to the car.

"Take me to her apartment," he tells the chauffeur as he is again seated, and the chauffeur steers the Mercedes out of the stadium and is about to head back to the main road. Another car is parked at the juncture of the stadium and its exit. Caseres sees the flags on the front fenders of the car.

"Stop when you are beside that car," he tells the chauffeur. Even before they are abreast of the car, Caseres sees Ambassador Nesbitt in the back seat.

When the chauffeur comes to a full stop beside the car, the rear window of his car and the rear window of the ambassador's car are opposite one another.

"Ambassador Nesbitt," says Caseres after rolling down his window, "are you out for some fresh air at this time of night?"

As a matter of fact I was following you," answers the ambassador. "I received a report from my colleague at the American Embassy in the country next door that might be of some interest to you. It's of great interest to me and to some of my superiors in Washington."

"Good news, I hope," says Caseres. He notices that the ambassador is not smiling.

"It seems that there was a military operation near the border today involving infantry and aircraft—*your* infantry and *your* aircraft."

"An internal matter, Mr. Ambassador."

"It seems that one of the planes used in this operation did not return. It also seems that some guerrillas in the area took a piece of the wing of that plane to the government next door. Your markings were clearly visible on the wing. It was equipment sent to you by the United States of America for defensive use only. And it also seems that it was shown on television there and then diffused internationally. And the reason I was following you was that I received earlier this evening a telex from Washington asking me for what is officially called 'clarification.'"

"What are you trying to tell me, Mr. Ambassador?"

"I'm trying to tell you that this is a serious matter and that my government is taking it most seriously. I tried to make myself and my government's position absolutely clear when we spoke earlier, but I now see that my words didn't make much of an impression. The fact of the matter is that my government is extremely disturbed that American equipment was used in what

your neighboring government's official television station called
an 'extermination raid.' The fact is that my government . . . "

"The fact is that your government can keep its mouth shut,
Mr. Ambassador," Caseres answers. His voice is rising as he
speaks. "The fact of the matter is that I am the only ally you have
in this part of the world, and you know it. You know it, and I
know it, and the whole world knows it. I am, if I may use the
word, unavoidable. In fact, I think that you are doing yourself a
favor by supplying me with military equipment because you realize you have no choice. There is no alternative, Mr. Ambassador.
There never has been, and there is none now."

"Premier Caseres, if I may finish what . . . "

"Let *me* finish, Ambassador Nesbitt," Caseres answers and
waits for Nesbitt to come to terms with the situation. "I don't
appreciate being tutored by you or that group of adolescents you
in your wisdom call a government." He waits for his words to
have their effect, then continues, "This is my country, and I
know what is good for my country. If I have good reason to
choose to use your sacred equipment, I'll use it, and I don't give
a damn whether the world knows about it or not. The great
United States of America may care about international opinion,
but, speaking for myself, I don't care enough about it even to piss
on it. Do you hear me? I piss on it. And after tomorrow my son
and I will both piss on it."

"I truly regret that you are of this disposition, Your Excellency. I particularly regret it because our relations, personal and
otherwise, have been so good for so long a period of time . . . "

"They will continue to be good, I assure you, Mr. Ambassador. And the reason they will continue to be good is that we
both need one another. I need your hardware and support at the
United Nations. You need my very presence here. I am totally
unavoidable. Remember that. And tell your president to remember that as well. I am unavoidable."

47

"DOESN'T HE REALIZE that he's insulting the United States of America?" shouts Nesbitt. His wife sits in bed with a martini in her hand, an audience of one to the tirade that he has kept going since returning from his meeting with Caseres at the stadium.

"You're working yourself into a heart attack over this. Why?" she asks.

"He's a son of a bitch. A genuine son of a bitch."

"All right, he's a son of a bitch. Does it make one bit of difference if you think he is?" She sets the martini on the bedside table and smiles to herself. "You know what our great white father would say to that if he heard you, don't you?"

"And what might that be?"

"He'd agree with everything you just said. And then he'd say in that casual original way of his, 'But he happens to be *our* son of a bitch.'"

"This is no time to be cute, Nell. We have a serious crisis here. And I'm the one who has to deal with it and report back about it, and I'm not looking forward to it at all."

Nesbitt's wife reaches for the martini, miscalculates the distance and knocks the drink to the floor.

"You're drinking too much, Nell," says Nesbitt as he picks shards of glass from the floor.

"I'll drink as much as I want, thank you, Mr. Ambassador," she answers tartly and swings her feet to the floor. When she tries to stand, she totters for a moment and then sits down heavily on the bed again. Her nightgown has edged up to her thighs, and Nesbitt notices as if for the first time how much weight she has gained. A varicose vein in her right leg is more evident that he remembered it to be. He deposits pieces of glass in a wastebasket by the bed as his wife manages to stand and make her way woodenly into the bathroom. She does not bother to close the door. A moment later he hears a thud. He runs into the bathroom and finds her on the floor, laughing.

"We must be having an earthquake," she says. "The floor moved when I tried to get off the commode."

"Let's get you off the floor, Nell. Did you hurt yourself?" He lifts her to her feet and steadies her for a moment. He sees that there is urine over the front of her nightgown.

"The floor's still moving," she says.

"Hold on to the sink for a minute, Nell. I have to get you out of this and into something dry."

"Oh, don't bother. I'm fine just the way I am."

He lifts the nightgown up her body and over her head.

"What are you doing?" she asks.

"Hold on to the sink," says Nesbitt, guiding her hand to the edge of the sink. "I'll be back in a minute."

She is standing exactly where he left her when he returns with a nightgown. For a moment he does not recognize her. He asks himself when it last was that he looked at her, *really* looked at her. Everything about her seems to have moved downward— her slack breasts, her lower belly, her hips. The smell of urine is still strong in the bathroom. He flushes the toilet before he moistens a washcloth with warm water from one of the sink taps and gently wipes her stomach and legs with it. Then he towels her dry.

"Yes sir, Mr. President," she is saying. "He is really *our* son of a bitch."

"That's enough for now, Nell."

He starts to slip the neck of the nightgown over her head, but she grabs it and throws it on floor.

"I'm sick of this. I'm sick and tired of this whole business," she screams. "I'm losing my mind in this damn country. I miss my children. I miss my grandchildren. What in the hell do I do here every day but get older and older? Do you want to know why I drink? That's why I drink. I can't accept the fact that this place is making an old woman out of me. Can you understand that?"

"We'll talk about it later, Nell," says Nesbitt, picking up the nightgown.

"We'll talk about it right now, Mister Goddamn Ambassador Nesbitt! Right now we'll talk about it!"

"Nell, stop it."

"No!"

"Well, then, just remember this ambassador thing was your idea in the first place. Everything would be okay if I had stayed in the business. I didn't have to get involved in this, but you kept urging me and urging until I thought it would be a good idea."

"There you go, blaming everything on me. What did I know? I'm not up on these things. I didn't know what it meant to be a goddamn diplomat."

"That's enough, Nell. I can . . . "

She is sobbing now, holding the sink edge with both hands and swaying back and forth. Then she starts to retch, and Nesbitt thinks she is going to vomit in the sink, but after a moment the retching eases.

He attempts to put the neck of her nightgown over her head again, and this time there is no resistance. Then he puts his arm around her waist and steers her cautiously back to her bed. She is so limp that she feels weightless against him, but he knows that she will collapse if he loosens his grip.

"Oh, Harry," she moans. "Get me out of here, Harry. Get me out of here, baby, before I do something terrible to myself. Please, Harry, please."

He feels such love for her then at that moment that he blinks back tears. He stops and embraces her, and for a minute or two they just stand in one another's arms in the middle of the room and keep holding each other desperately as if their very lives depended on it.

"I'll get you out of this, Nell," he whispers, kissing her on her forehead. "I'll get you out of this, and we'll go back home. I'll take you home with me."

"Please, baby," she whimpers. "I can't take it any more. I just can't, honest to God."

He helps her to bed. She is now weeping without check. When he has her under the covers and has bunched the pillow under her head, he sits on the bed beside her and holds her hand.

"I'm so sorry, Harry," she says after she is calm. "I'm sorry if I was the one who got you into this. Things didn't turn out the way I thought they would. I'm sorry."

"Forget it, Nell. It was as much my fault as yours."

"I'll make it up to you, Harry."

"There's nothing to make up. You just lie back and try to get some sleep."

She closes her eyes and grips his hand more tightly. He studies the tear paths on her cheeks. He knows without a doubt that he will write his letter of resignation in the morning. But before that he will have to report his version of his confrontation with Caseres in the stadium to his superiors in the State Department. He resigns himself to the fact that he will have to weather the consequences. Then he wonders if they will accept his resignation as long as American relations with Caseres are unresolved. He imagines that he might even be ordered to stay on post to keep from bringing further attention to the situation. He has long since learned that governments are most sensitive to unanticipated embarrassment than to anything else. But how long would he have to remain on post? Weeks? Months? Half a year?

48

MAGDALENA HAS JUST FINISHED washing her face when she hears the precise stop of Caseres' Mercedes. She dabs a towel around her eyepits and then across the back of her neck. She folds the towel lengthwise, hangs it over its rack, and listens to Caseres as he turns the key in the lock. When she emerges from the bathroom, he is standing in the hallway waiting for her. He holds open his arms, and she permits herself to be embraced and kissed once on the cheek.

"Clean," says Caseres. "You smell so clean, Magdalena." He kisses her again but this time on her mouth.

She slides slowly away from him and walks into the living room where she lights a cigarette.

"I thought I told you not to smoke," says Caseres, crossing in front of her and taking his usual seat by the window.

"It gives me something to do with my hands."

"But smoking is not good for your voice."

"You know I'm not singing much any more."

"But you sing for me. I am an audience of one, and you will always sing for me." He smiles and adds, "What if I ask you to sing my special song at the stadium tomorrow?"

"It's not the right occasion."

"If I say it's the right occasion, then it is the right occasion."

"Do you say so?"

"I say so."

Magdalena shrugs and snuffs out the cigarette in an ashtray.

"People will never forget tomorrow, Magdalena," continues Caseres. "It will be a spectacle worthy of Pompeii. Let me show you how it will be." He places his foot in the center of the rug beside his chair. "I will be here where my foot is. The elite corps will be here to my right." He shifts his foot slightly. "The musicians and the drummers here." He moves his foot again. "The foreign representatives will be behind the musicians and the drummers, and the people—*my* people—will fill the stadium. Each person will have a flag in his hand."

"And Radames?"

"Beside me, of course. The whole spectacle is for him. It will be his anointing."

"Perhaps you should have invited his mother." Magdalena's tone is mock-serious.

Caseres waves his hand as if he might be brushing away a fly. "She is part of the past, and tomorrow is dedicated to the future, Magdalena. She does not exist in that future. There is nothing for her here. The only good thing she ever did was to give me Radames, and for that she has a $10 million reward in the Bank of Locarno for the rest of her life. The interest on that figure alone should be more than enough for her to live like a queen until she dies."

"Do you still think of her?"

"Think of her? I wouldn't have mentioned her name now if you hadn't brought it up. I have more important matters to think about." He pauses and looks out the window. "Today we crushed them, Magdalena."

Magdalena waits for an explanation.

"Do you remember the village I mentioned to you yesterday, the one that has been like a nail in my shoe for all these years?"

"Megiddo?"

"Yes, Megiddo. It is finished. There is no more Megiddo. Nothing is left of it, and no one who was in it is still alive. My soldiers and my pilots turned it into powder. Nothing is there but death. There were no survivors, and not a building is still standing." He pauses. "It cost me some of my best men, but it was worth it. It was more heavily defended than we thought. They surprised us. But now it is history. Gone. Finished."

"Does that make you happy?"

"It relieves me, and that makes me happy."

"Good."

Magdalena takes the ashtray into the kitchen and shakes the snuffed butt and the ashes into the wastebasket. Before she returns to Caseres, she notices the morning mail that she has left unexamined on the kitchen table. Fingering through a few flyers and magazines, she comes upon a lone letter. She instantly recognizes her brother's handwriting.

"Magdalena," Caseres calls from the other room.

"Yes."

"We are wasting time, Magdalena."

"One moment. I am coming," she answers as she slits open the envelope with her fingernail and removes and unfolds the letter. She tilts it toward the light and reads . . . "here in the village. All the people here know about you and the premier. They say things about you that are insults. The insults are more than I can stand, and I am sure that our mother has heard them, but she says nothing. Today I am going to join Father Sabertes in Megiddo. Caseres plans to send his men against Megiddo soon, and Father Sabertes says that there will be a resistance. I have decided I cannot live unless I do something against Caseres and everything he has done to you and to us. I am doing this for you, Magdalena . . . " She drops the letter.

"Magdalena!"

She retrieves the letter and crumples it beside the ashes in the wastebasket. Then she returns to the living room where Caseres is standing beside his chair. He has already loosened his tie and opened the collar of his shirt. He then sits down and removes his boots and stands them at attention side by side near the chair. When he finishes, he looks at her and extends his hand to her.

"You are looking at me like a lioness, Magdalena."

"No," she answers. "I was thinking of what you said about Megiddo."

"Megiddo is no more. It is over."

"But what about the people who lived there? What about the rebels you said were there? Are they prisoners now?"

"Prisoners?"

"Yes. Were there any prisoners taken at Megiddo?"

"No prisoners. My orders. The mission would have been a failure if there had been one survivor. I wanted no one left alive to tell the story." He reaches for her hand and starts to pull her toward him, but she backs away. "We are wasting time, Magdalena."

"Bathroom . . . forgot something." She frees her hand. "Wait for me." She retreats into the bathroom, shuts the door and leans against it. She is perspiring, but her mouth and lips are completely dry. She goes to the cabinet and opens it. She spots the safety razor that she uses on her legs, removes it and unscrews the top flanges to release the blade. But there is no blade. Then she remembers having disposed of it the previous week. She sorts through various bottles, medicines, and boxes, but she finds no razor blades, used or unused. She returns to the door and opens it. Caseres is standing no more than a few feet away.

"You are playing games, Magdalena."

"No, no, I'm not. I just need a few minutes, please. A woman is not like a man. A woman has preparations to make. Be patient. It will be better for you, I promise." Again she closes the door and hears Caseres return to his chair in the living room. Because he is between her and the kitchen, she knows that she cannot reach the kitchen where the carving knives are. His view of her there would be unobstructed. Almost panting, she sits on the rim of the bathtub. After a few moments she seems calmer, and a different look comes into her eyes. She takes a deep breath, stands, and walks toward the mirror. After removing the clips from her hair, she brushes it straight back so that it reaches her shoulder blades. Then she applies henna deftly to her eyes, and expertly traces the outlines of her lips with lipstick. With an eyebrow pencil, she thickens the lines of her eyebrows and extends them. Then she dabs cologne behind her eyes and between her breasts. When she is finished, she removes her dress, underwear, and shoes and puts on a beige nightgown she left hanging from a hook behind the door. She examines herself in the mirror one last time, turns off the light and leaves the bathroom.

Caseres does not hear her come up behind him. When he does, he turns, studies her, and smiles. "Now," he says, "now I can see why you wanted me to wait, Magdalena."

"I knew you wouldn't regret waiting a few moments. You knew I wouldn't disappoint you."

He reaches for her and puts his arms around her waist. She leans forward and kisses him on the forehead, letting the scent and sway of her breasts reach him. She stays that way for a moment longer and then takes his hand and leads him to her bedroom. She does not hurry, making sure that her body touches his as they walk.

Once they are near the bed, she makes him sit down and helps him removes his shirt.

"My pills," he says, "don't forget my pills in my shirt pocket."

She unbuttons the pocket and removes the small vial and places it on the nightstand. Then she eases him face up on the bed. She removes his socks and the rest of his clothes, letting him watch her all the while, letting her brushed hair skim his body, letting his fingers brush her nipples and the soft swells of her inner thighs. Then she stands in the light and pulls the nightgown in one slow lift over her head and lets it fall behind her. She knows he is watching her, and she lets him taste her fully with his eyes.

When she turns to dim the lamp, she does it slowly so that he can see her from many different angles as she moves. In the semidarkness she can hear him breathing heavily from the bed, something he always does when he is aroused.

"Magdalena," he says, "you are an orchid."

She sits on the edge of the bed and slides her hands softly over his chest, his waist, his legs, and back to his chest. At last she touches him where he enjoys most being touched, adjusting herself so that her breasts are against him and her cheek is flush against his chest. He is breathing more rapidly now, but the heaviness has not gone away. With her cheek against him, she can hear the deep, sluggish pump of his heart.

Still touching him, she mounts him and feels him thrust upward at her groin, but she does not lower herself on him.

"Magdalena," he says. It is more of an utterance than a word.

She continues to weave her hips just out of range of him, letting him touch her but not enter her. He is breathing now as if there is a knot of phlegm in his throat. She sits back on his knees, then slides full length beside him and draws him against her. She kisses him on the cheeks and then on the mouth. She draws her tongue over his lips and eyelashes. She lets her legs yawn apart so that he can touch her freely, and she can feel him throbbing against her each time her loins contact his. Then she pulls away from him. He reaches across the bed for her. She takes his hands and puts his palms on her breasts.

"Now, Magdalena," he says. As before, it is an utterance.

After he rolls on his back, she mounts him a second time. Her pubis finds him, then eludes, finds him, then eludes.

"Magdalena . . . "

She eludes him a moment longer before she lets him penetrate her, but it is just for a second. She pulls up. Caseres starts to cough as if the phlegm-like knot in his throat is gagging him. Magdalena keeps letting her pubis touch him so that Caseres, even while he coughs, is still thrusting into her. Finally, the cough become a deep retch, and Caseres gags one, two, three, four times before he mutters, "Mag-da-lena . . . pills . . . my pills . . . give them to me . . ."

Still straddling him, Magdalena reaches for the vial of pills. Caseres is breathing now as if every breath requires a separate act of his will. Between her thighs Magdalena can feel his body tighten and convulse every time he sucks in a breath.

"The pills . . . now . . . I need them . . ."

He reaches up toward her, but she parries his hands. His hands are quivering, his palms are cold, and he is breathing now like a man about to drown.

Magdalena flings the vial across the room and leans over Caseres until her face is just over his. He keeps trying to turn over or work free, but her straddle keeps him centered on the bed. He is fully extended inside of her now, and she squeezes him there tightly. When he tries to withdraw, she squeezes him harder, locking him within her. Then she seizes his hair with both hands so that his head is fixed against the bed.

"Mag-da . . ."

Before he can finish saying her name, she covers his mouth with her own, pressing down on him so that she can feel his teeth against her teeth. He flails at her with both arms, but the strength has long since gone out of them, and they flop backward on the bed like broken wings. She listens to the phlegmy chug of his breath. Each time he tries to wrench away from her, she clenches her fingers more tightly and pulls his hair taut. Finally, she actually bites into his lips so that he cannot close his mouth. It is as if she is sucking the breath out of him, pinning him with her body and her hands until there is one final convulsion and then a limpness so total that Magdalena feels as if Caseres has somehow diminished beneath her. But she continues to hold him by the hair and bite into his slackening mouth for a moment longer before she releases him and sits up. Her legs are shaking from the strain, and the sweat from her hair and neck is sliding down her back and between her breasts like oil. She wipes her mouth with the back of her forearm, dismounts, and stands beside the bed. She gropes for her nightgown on the floor and puts it on. Then she turns on the light and stares at Caseres. His dead eyes are staring straight up at the ceiling. His mouth is wide open and sagging slightly to the right. The marks of her teeth have left crimson dents on his upper lip. His arms are outstretched in a limp crucifixion.

Magdalena turns away, walks into the bathroom, and with a moist washrag wipes her mouth, her hands, and then her groin. When she returns to Caseres, she looks up his length from his now totally listless legs, past the slack genitals and the diminished chest to the bulging eyes. She stands quietly for several moments. Her face has the expression of a woman who is expecting nothing, hoping for nothing, planning for nothing. Then she makes the sign of the cross by touching Caseres on his forehead, chest, and both shoulders with her right hand. When she finishes, she wipes her hands on the sheet.

Ten minutes later she walks to the front door, opens it, and descends the stairs to the stoop where Caseres' chauffeur is smoking a cigarette. As soon as the chauffeur sees her, he guiltily throws away the cigarette and stands. She beckons him closer with her eyes. He looks at her curiously for a moment and then steps toward her.

"The premier," she says slowly when the chauffeur is in front of her, "the premier has had an attack. There was nothing I could do. It happened all at once. Go up to him."

49

LUBO IS SITTING BEHIND A TABLE on which three micro-
phones have been placed side by side. He blinks as seven pho-
tographers repeatedly take his picture. Standing with pens and
pencils hovering over their pads, a dozen reporters are poised a
few yards in front of the table.

"Do you have anything to add?" asks one of the reporters.

"No," says Lubo. "I've shown you the evidence. It was American equipment that was used, and it was used illegally on our own
people. We went through all that last night."

"What do you think will happen now that Premier Caseres is
dead?" asks a second reporter.

"What do *you* think will happen?"

"That doesn't answer my question."

"Then you should never have asked . . . " Lubo pauses as a
messenger enters the room and whispers something to an older
reporter who seems to be the senior journalist present. The
reporter looks somewhat surprised, and the messenger nods his
head in the affirmative.

"This man has just brought me news that puts a different
light on everything," says the older reporter. "He told me that
the body of Radames has just been found floating in the sea near
his villa. And they've located his car in the water as well. The
assumption is that his car apparently went off the road. Either he
lost control . . . "

"Radames?" asks Lubo.

"Yes."

"And he is dead as well?" Lubo persists. "Are they sure it was Radames?"

The older reporter turns to the messenger, who again nods a slow and solemn yes. All the reporters are silent, and Lubo looks at each of them, waiting for the next question.

"What have the Americans said about this matter?" Lubo asks finally.

"Ambassador Nesbitt announced after he learned of the death of Caseres that the American government would be willing to cooperate with Radames as the legitimate successor to his father."

"But now there is no Radames," says Lubo.

"He meant that the American government would be willing to work with any government here that would remain neutral in this part of the world," the older reporter says.

Lubo nods but says nothing.

"Do you have any comment on Ambassador Nesbitt's statement?" asks the older reporter.

"What does that have to do with me?"

"Well, your name has been mentioned for years now as someone who might run the country some day. Maybe that day has arrived."

"I'll have no comment on that now."

"We know that you have the support of the villagers as well as the rank and file in the army. Isn't that enough of a mandate for you to consider taking a position about this?"

"I've been a guerrilla fighter for seven years. I cannot become political overnight."

"But you have an uncle who is political . . . who was political."

"My uncle was political, yes. He was a great orator, but he was imprisoned by Caseres. And when he was exiled to France, Caseres made sure he would never speak again."

"But now might be the time when you can speak for him."

One of the younger reporters steps forward. He waits for a nod from the older reporter before he says, "Seven years is a long time to carry on your kind of resistance. Surely you must have had support from within the country. Financial support, I mean."

"No financial support from within the country. All we had was the knowledge that the people were fed up with Caseres."

"Did you receive funds from outside the country?"

"Yes, we received funds."

"From any government you might care to name now?"

"Not from any government," Lubo answers. "Our funds came from a private source."

"Would you care to name the source?"

"Someone in Paris."

"Who in Paris?"

Lubo shrugs and says, "I don't know. The funds came every month. In the beginning it was French francs. Then it was dollars."

"In other words, currency."

"Currency, yes."

"Anonymously?"

"Anonymously. When you need money, you don't ask and you don't care where it comes from."

"But how did you get it? Did someone bring it?"

"It came by mail in a parcel to my uncle's home."

"The uncle who is in exile in Paris?"

"Yes, his daughter still lives here. A note inside the first parcel instructed her to deliver it to me. And she did."

"So you received the money from your cousin?"

"Yes."

"And you never found out who was sending it?"

"We tried. The closest we came was when we traced the francs. We learned that the donor was a woman—definitely a woman. We traced it to a specific section on the Right Bank, then to the Boulevard des Grands Augustin, but the trail ended there. After that my cousin delivered a certified package of dollars every month from the Bank of Locarno. But we could find out nothing. The Swiss protect their investors, as you know. Their confidentiality is like the seal of the confessional. But over the years those francs and later the dollars made our resistance to Caseres possible from the first of our attacks to the battle in Megiddo." He pauses. "Without that help there would have been no resistance, no Megiddo, no alternative to Caseres, nothing."